To

W.T.A. PITMAN

Never forgotten.

Contents

CHAPTER 1

The Gatekeeper burst through the gates of eternal fire which imprisoned his collection of restless souls. With his thread-bare cloak still smouldering from the demonic inferno, he charged through the valley of the perished who screamed and wailed on each side of the walkway. The constant bone-chilling moans would strike fear in even the bravest of men, but the Gatekeeper was an Elder; an Elder who was charged with the decision between life and death.

In pure desperation, one of the souls dived forward stretching as far it could reach within the limits of its flaming ankle-chain, clawing at his master's cloak. A cockroach scurried from within the cloak and crawled over the flickering soul's face. The decaying remains of The Gatekeeper's right hand sent a cracking noise resonating around the sizzling cavern walls as he gripped the wooden handle of his scythe.

With a lightning-quick thrust, the razor-sharp weapon sliced straight through the shadowy monstrosity and with a final cry the creature evaporated into the air. The fiery chains that had held the creature clattered to the stone floor. Even though the flames were extinguished, they continued to glow red-hot, before they were dragged back into the darkness.

Forcing his cloak to the side and returning his attention to his grand mirror, the Gatekeeper approached the glassy surface and with his touch it vibrated and hummed, opening a portal to the world of man.

Far below, lay the majestic Castle of Sepura. The imposing drawbridge opened, and the Gatekeeper watched as the four children of evil knelt, the Sixes on their arms glowing as they awaited their prize. Talula, Harry, Percy and Jimmy, all kneeling, were lost in a deep trance.

The creature of darkness snarled, grinding his teeth in anger. "Lyreco, you dare blame me for the death of Bill Threepwood? And you, pathetic, meek Jimmy Threepwood, you dare challenge my power? This is a battle you will not win!" he roared.

The Gatekeeper gave a sinister laugh and with a snap of his left arm wrapped his spindly fingers around the throat of the closest wailing soul. The unsuspecting soul squealed as the Gatekeeper thrust it high into the air, its ankle-chain snapping under the pressure as the soul was forced against the mirror's surface. The Gatekeeper looked at the shadowy creature. The two exchanged an intense gaze as the memories from the soul's former, mortal life drained into its tormentor's twisted mind.

"Yes, you are the one I was looking for." The Gatekeeper scowled. "I have a job for you, my prisoner. If you succeed, you will be given a second chance at life. Do you wish to know what you have to do?"

The soul's eyes flickered around the cavern before it nodded giving out a pathetic squeal. It didn't care what it had to do; it would do anything to escape this world of nightmares.

Squirming, still groaning from the tight grip around its neck, the soul received its orders telepathically. Thrusting his skeletal arm through the warped mirror the Gatekeeper cast the soul through a tear in the fabric of the world, before sending the soul hurtling downward toward Sepura Castle.

The soul tumbled through the atmosphere, burning white-hot like a meteor. It tore through the clouds towards the wooden drawbridge, which was opening slowly below as the ground beneath grew closer and closer. The four unsuspecting chosen ones knelt nearby.

*   *   *

Plummeting over the heads of the children, a gust of air ruffled Jimmy's hair. The soul crashed into the water with an almighty splash, jolting Jimmy Threepwood from his trance. Jimmy rose to his feet, shaking his head to clear the cobwebs and gather his bearings. He glanced around and realised that his companions were still under the spell of the Amulet of Trident.

Creeping past the group to investigate what had landed in the water, Jimmy grabbed onto the rotten wooden railing and peered over the edge. He expected crystal-clear water, but instead saw a drifting sea of thick black sludge. Dozens of tiny bubbles formed and popped, releasing a foul green gas into the air. Looking closer, Jimmy saw thousands of white spirits drifting aimlessly. A wave of menacing clear-white faces stared back up at him.

Jimmy was mesmerised by the calming flow of the sea when suddenly something sharp bit at his finger. Pulling back his hand sharply he saw a tiny wooden splinter lodged in his index finger. Jimmy put his finger in his mouth and tried to suck out the tiny piece of wood.

Still concentrating on his finger Jimmy turned back to the sea and flinched as he saw a wild demonic face staring back at him. The flickering black face screamed at Jimmy, its yellow piercing eyes empty, its black flickering fangs dripping a foul tar substance which stuck to the wooden railing. Jimmy reacted without thinking, but the creature's reflexes were like lightning. The creature thrust its black, razor sharp talons forward and around Jimmy's throat, forcing him to stagger backwards across the creaking bridge. Jimmy sank his hands into the creature's tar-covered wrists and pushed with all his might. For the first time he could see the hatred in the creature's eyes, but it wasn't hatred for him. Jimmy was just in the wrong place.

The struggle continued, and Jimmy used all his strength to wrench the claws away from his neck. He didn't realise he was moving backwards until he felt the opposite wooden railing wobble behind him. The creature gave an ear-piercing screech, spraying Jimmy's face with the tar. With one more thrust, the rotten wood behind Jimmy snapped, sending them both tumbling into the black sea.

Even after the fall, the creature was relentless. It forced Jimmy down into the depths of the water.

Jimmy started to panic. He was unable to breathe and released his grip from the abomination's wrists. Desperately he tried to punch the ghoul, but his fist had lost its power in the water and it hit the thick, syrupy texture without effect. Jimmy sunk past the white spirits floating in the water, each one knocking more breath from his lungs.

Jimmy was turning blue and his vision was beginning to blur. Tiny purple stars appeared before his eyes. His throat was on fire. It burnt like he had swallowed lava as he choked. He could hear his heart banging like a distant drum in his chest. The instant before he passed out, he saw a vision staring back at him: a translucent mirror image of himself outlined within the water. The mirror image swam towards Jimmy from behind the flickering black creature, grabbing the black soul and yanking it off Jimmy's neck. The image kicked the creature away before pulling Jimmy upward toward the surface.

Slowly the world grew dark.

"Jimmy ... Jimmy," a distant voice called. Opening his eyes Jimmy was surrounded by complete blackness. When his eyes had adjusted, he saw the outline of a tunnel and in the distance, he could just about make out the shape of a golden owl flapping its wings flying closer and closer towards him. As it approached, words echoed throughout his mind.

"Jimmy, you are different, you know it. You must help us. You must search out Higuain."

An image was flashed into his mind's eye of a beautiful long-haired woman. A sweet aroma of midnight jasmine swirled around his body and tantalised his senses, filling him with warmth.

"Two days' time, two o'clock, Black Friars Alley. Searrrrrch the library and bring her the Scroll of the Granite Fairies."

Someone reached out and gripped Jimmy's collar, pulling him to the surface and dragging him onto a floating wooden panel. He inhaled fresh air, coughing as though it was his last breath. He heard a splash. Rings of water rippled around him but whoever had saved him was gone. He collapsed drawing every breath he could into his lungs.

*   *   *

The flickering black soul barged past the white, lifeless spirits floating in the black sea. Seeing the grassy bank, the creature thrust its right claw out of the water, digging it into the foliage and mud before dragging its other arm then its head out. The creature stared down at its dripping, black claw. Exposed to the clean mortal air, away from its deathly prison, the claw had changed into a human hand. The inky black liquid drained away into the water. The creature squealed, revealing its fangs as its other hand and then its head slowly returned to human form. The half-human, half-demonic-parasite lifted itself onto the bank. The covering of thick tar, oozed away. His body returned to how it used to be; he was once more a brown-bearded man—a form he had not seen since that night …

He rubbed his fingers over the rough texture of his thick green tunic, then lifted his head as he heard the cry of a horse in the near distance. Tearing himself away from his memories he saw a man holding a black-winged stallion. A man he had not seen in a long, long time.

*   *   *

On the far side of the bridge, Lyreco and Xanadu had managed to regain control of the mystical, newly formed Virorapters, flapping their bat-like wings and dragging their hooves across the dusty floor. Lyreco noticed the damaged wooden railing on the bridge and out of the corner of his eye he saw a flicker of movement, and a bearded male with long, brown scraggly hair darting into the undergrowth.

Hellsby? thought Lyreco. *It can't be. You were taken centuries ago.* He ran shaking fingers through his tatty beard.

CHAPTER 2

A lone fly buzzed through the thunderous storm, battered and blown around in the violent air. Blinking its many eyes, it saw a distant, ancient museum with a shining light burning through a window.

The drenched fly dropped through a small gap in a steel vent and darted along the sterile halls in search of the light. Circling the musty chamber, the insect settled on the golden weapon of a decaying Egyptian warrior.

Heavy rain thumped on the small glass window above, echoing throughout the room of history as the tiny fly blinked its many eyes.

*   *   *

"Higuain, I've done all I can for Argon," said the softly-spoken water healer, Dravid. His voice filled with concern. "He was very weak and so old. I don't know how he survived this long, but he will never be able to leave the eclipse portal the way he is." Higuain walked past the four stone hibernation capsules to the one that had been freshly sealed containing the golden-haired Argon. Lovingly, she ran her fingers over the stone animation machine, remembering.

Ignoring the memories that threatened to engulf her, defiant words leapt from her mouth.

"No! there must be a way. Argon survived an *apocalypse* and *two thousand years to keep us safe* and to make sure the prophecy never happens again. I will never give up on him. There must be a way … somehow. For now, at least the eclipse capsule will keep him safe locked in a time loop, not aging any further. We need to secure the other capsules then come up with some form of plan to help Argon and find a way to put an end to Tyranacus—once and for all."

Dravid stood next to the museum alarm system and prodded the keyboard of the office computer. "They are not as advanced this time around," Dravid shouted. "Their computers are very primitive. They are still encased in plastic and do not form a suitable human holographic image to provide answers. They are still using electricity in their lighting and power systems. It seems they have yet to harness the power of the earth's core as an unlimited power source."

The wild, fiery-haired warrior, Stratos, interrupted Dravid, roaring before propping his axe against the wall.

"I had the beast beaten!" he growled, still furious how the last battle had ended two thousand years ago forcing the Light Dwellers into centuries of hiding. "Tyranacus was at my mercy and we were winning until that witch Aurabella blasted me from behind. Where did she come from? The children of Tyranacus were all injured and on the floor. Anyway, it shows the beast is vulnerable when it is first released, when it is still forming. We must think of a way of defeating it then. That's our best chance."

*　　　*　　　*

Dravid turned away from the mighty Stratos, having seen the burns which were still clearly visible on his back even after all this time. No-one knew it was he that had helped the injured Lady Aurabella during the battle, and of course, she had gone on to strike down Stratos as he was about to administer the final, fatal blow to save the world.

*   *   *

"No!" snapped Higuain. "We tried that last time and Tyranacus still managed to beat us. It is too powerful and too dangerous. What if the same thing happens again? No, we will defeat the children whilst they are young and prevent it happening at all, it's the only way."

Stratos thumped the thick stone wall of the museum in anger. The strike shook the foundations and his colossal axe slipped and fell to the ground with a clank.

Dravid shook his hea. "That type of behaviour will get us … what's that?" he said in mid-sentence. His eyes dropped to the floor. "Look. The axe has knocked Argon's walking cane over. There's something poking out. It looks like paper."

Dravid used the tips of his fingers and delicately pinched the end of the crumbling paper from the cane; he pulled out a tightly rolled note. 'This must have been in there for years. Look, the paper is completely brown. It feels bone-dry."

Dravid took his time unravelling the note and cleared his throat.

My dear, dear friends,

If you have found this, it must be too late for me. I've wandered this lifeless, empty world alone for far too long.

It's gone. It is all gone. Those creatures destroyed everything. The trees are destroyed, and the sky is burnt -

constantly glowing an angry red. The heavens rain smouldering fire and ash, and the water is alight with fire. I can't see how it can ever heal itself, I don't know if I can go on.

You, my friends, are now the only hope for mankind this time around. You must stop Tyranacus and the apocalypse. This disaster, this pain and suffering must never happen again.

But if I survive long enough to release you, there may be a chance for me.

Whilst wandering the earth I remembered a rare flower called a Palletine. This contains the blood of Velosaras.

Even the tiniest drop will heal any injury and if taken correctly, will even reverse the effects of time and age.

I know of this flower, as it was used by the children bearing the mark of Tyranacus.

It helped to stop their skin decaying from the overuse of dark magic.

Once taken by the children it will also enhance their powers, unleashing stronger and longer-lasting spells.

Find the flower, it is our only hope. But be wary, the children will soon start their quest to find it.

Yours longingly,

Argon Monteith.

Higuain wiped tears from her eyes and couldn't get the thought out of her mind of her only love spending eternity walking through that hell alone. "He must have been so scared, but he is brave," she whispered. "Right, we must have found this note for a reason. We will find this flower if it is the last thing we do. We will help him, like he helped us."

"What if it no longer exists?" asked Dravid. "What if the flower became extinct when the world was destroyed?"

"A flower like that wouldn't die. It must be somewhere as the children will also need it to survive. If we don't find it, Argon will not survive."

A whip of yellow lightning flashed through the night sky. The tiny fly flapped its wings and flew off out of the museum.

*   *   *

Lyreco stared down at the snapped railing. "Something has gone wrong at the castle. I cannot see Jimmy."

Xanadu began tugging at Lyreco's sleeve like a small child. "What is it, Xanadu?" he barked.

"Master, master," said Xanadu, "the spy has returned with information."

The tiny fly flapped its wings and landed on the tip of Xanadu's protruding tongue. With one gulp, the greasy, black-haired goblin ate the fly. Her eyes turned green and her body became rigid.

Without expression or emotion Xanadu opened her mouth.

"This (*buzz*) is the recording of the group you asked me to find (*buzz*). The recording will begin in ten seconds (*buzz*), nine …"

Using Xanadu's body as a speaker system, the insect spy relayed the story of the note and the magical flower. Lyreco listened intently. Once the story finished Xanadu gulped and with a shake of her head returned to her normal grotesque self.

"So, they do live after all," said Lyreco. "I thought that traitor died a long time ago with his pathetic army. They also know about the flower. Well, no matter, we will just have to find it first. Come, we must act quickly."

CHAPTER 3

Jimmy coughed opening his eyes. He was drifting in the water on a panel of wood. He pulled himself further onto it and using his arms, paddled through the current of white spirits before reaching the rushes. Jimmy dragged himself onto the bank and pulled off his soaking cloak, which squelched as it splattered onto the floor. He smoothed back his wet hair and wiped the treacle-like water off his face. Then he looked at his companions. They were still locked in a trance, unaware of Jimmy's struggle. Lyreco was also gone.

*   *   *

The drawbridge locked into place with a crunch. Talula, Harry and Percy awoke as one from their trance and rose, disorientated. They didn't even notice that Jimmy wasn't with them. They were so enthused with the prospect of finally finding unlimited power they were unable to contain their excitement as they ran off, disappearing into the entrance of the dark castle, led by Percy.

*   *   *

Jimmy's feet sploshed inside his soaking boots as he picked up his sodden robes, tucked them under his arm and followed the others, having watched them awaken and charge into the castle before he had a chance to shout to them. As Jimmy walked along he left a trail of wet, syrupy footprints on the wooden drawbridge. Jimmy picked up his pace and re-joined the group behind Talula.

The four children crossed the threshold into the cold, damp castle and their nostrils were hit by thin, stale air. It held the indisputable smell of decay and burnt flesh, which had been sealed inside for centuries. They covered their noses with their sleeves and looked beyond, unable to stand still through excitement.

Jimmy stepped forward onto the hard floor, but as he applied pressure, one of the stone slabs sank under his weight. The sound of stone scraping against stone echoed through the vast castle as one by one, a thousand floating green flames danced into life, sending light into every corner. Talula, Harry, Percy and Jimmy stood gawking in astonishment.

A floor composed of black and white square tiles led into a highly-polished entrance hall. It could have been very grand, scattered with rare and valuable items, but everything was encased in layers of thick cobwebs. Two rows of elegant columns reached from floor to ceiling on either side, framing a path down the centre of the room. In a prominent position at the far side was a peculiar staircase with emerald-coloured steps. The steps were made of what looked like marble and had gold coloured railings, but there were only six steps and they didn't appear to go anywhere.

On either side of the entrance were two black doors - each with a purple, wobbling, diamond-shaped window. The children approached the centre of the room, and a circle of six green lights arranged around the edge of the hall suddenly burst to life. Each light projected a five second moving image, depicting what Jimmy supposed must be monumental moments from history. He realised that the motion clips were being projected from tiny lenses embedded in the tiles.

The first clip showed Sepura Castle in all its glory and an unusual giant white saucer shaped platform lodged deep within the east wing.

The second clip displayed the area around the castle. As far as the eye could see it was surrounded by pure blue water. The saucer started to spin, casting a rainbow of colours into the air. Enormous areas of the water solidified, turning brown then green as patches of grass grew, and vast fields expanded in front of their very eyes. In the wake of the shadow of colour, mountains formed, trees grew, and the new world radiated— ready to prosper.

Talula gasped as a third clip began. It depicted a circular world covered in thick black smog withering and coming to the end of its existence. A demonic human face filled with rage grew from within the smog; screaming silently ...

In the next clip, four hooded warriors stood in a circle within the fog, drenched in acid rain as wild thunderstorms and tsunamis raged around them. With a surge of immense white light, a huge red-skinned demon burst out of the decaying ground and roared, thrashing a glistening black axe.

The next projection brought them crashing to reality. The creature, accompanied by four blue-winged abominations on horseback, savaged the world, destroying man, buildings and the land.

The last clip was the worst of them all ... seas of fire, skies dripping with blood and thick black ash rained down through smoky fog, day and night. Only a handful would survive.

The visions of the past severely affected the children as they finally saw what they must do ... what they would do.

An eerie, raspy voice spoke behind them. "Evening, my new masters. Welcome to your new home."

The group jumped in fright. They turned to see a bald, gaunt-faced man with deeply sunken eyes.

"Who are you?" asked Talula.

"Please, don't be alarmed," the man spoke again, his voice deep and booming. "I am the butler of this splendid castle, my name is Majordomo."

Harry could barely tear his eyes away from the man's disfigured face. The man's skin was thin and lifeless, but it was also badly burnt and scarred under both cheeks. Yellow teeth appeared through the damaged and broken flesh. Each breath was a struggle for the butler, who wheezed and rasped with every intake of air. It sounded like he had water on his lungs. As Majordomo closed his eyes for a moment the full extent of his poor health was evident.

The lanky man towered over the children and pulled the torn black gown closer around his withered body. Jimmy studied him carefully and was surprised to see thin, webbed metal talons instead of feet.

"You will be wishing to see your rooms? They are ready and waiting for you." Majordomo inhaled deeply as though it was his last breath through a ventilation machine. Slightly parting his cloak, he lifted a white-gloved hand and beckoned. There was an awkward silence.

"No luggage? Hmm," he groaned in displeasure. "Your stay here will be most unpleasant. I will fetch you a new set of robes. Once you have been to your rooms you will be allowed to explore the grounds. However, you are not allowed access to every room. Only certain doors will open. Please follow me up the emerald staircase."

The butler turned and walked off, each step clanking on the marble, chequered floor.

Percy considered the six-stepped staircase in the centre of the room, shrugged his shoulders and followed the ancient hunched-over ghoul towards their rooms.

Jimmy was last to follow and curiously walked to a black door situated to the left of the entrance he had seen when they first entered the castle. He touched the thick, cold wood, and noticed that there was no door handle or key hole. He stood on tip toes and peered through the purple wobbling window.

A vicious face appeared on the other side, screaming at Jimmy, causing him to take a step back in surprise. The face mellowed and Jimmy approached the window once more. He lifted a finger to touch it. The face snapped his teeth as a warning and Jimmy pulled away. Snarling, the voice spoke.

"Jiiiiimmmyy Thhreeeeppwoood, I am Lorda. Guardian of this room. There will be no admittance until you are ready. Begone!"

Lorda pressed his face into the window and the strange wobbling liquid stretched around his features. The image then turned and walked away deeper into the diamond shaped glass, sitting down on a chair in front of a roaring fire.

It looks like a classroom! Jimmy thought, glancing around the room and noting the chairs and desks lined perfectly in rows.

"Jimmy!" snapped Majordomo. "Your room."

Jimmy pulled away from the window. He glanced back, a cast of his face remained within the diamond for a few seconds before it rippled and returned to normal.

Talula, Harry and Percy each stood on a different step on the staircase. Jimmy apprehensively stepped onto the bottom one and waited in anticipation.

"This, my new masters, is the emerald staircase. You must each stand on a different step, unless, you are, of course, going to the same room. You merely have to think about your location and you will be transported there. Talula, you are in room five. Please, think about the room."

Talula seemed uneasy but closed her eyes and steadied her breathing. Instantly her step hummed, turning to jelly. Slowly Talula sank through the floor. Then she was gone.

Fascinated, the others quickly received their room numbers and descended through their steps too.

As a parting message, Majordomo commanded, "The Council of Elders have requested your presence, Jimmy Threepwood. I will collect you when they are ready." Jimmy stepped onto his step, thought of his room number and vanished.

CHAPTER 1

Jimmy sank through the ceiling of a stone bedroom and landed on the bed. He was exhausted after his adventures, so he sank his head into the softest pillow and studied the dark, lifeless room. It was a basic room with a small bed, wooden table, wardrobe and a mirror hanging on the wall. The dark purple walls did nothing to improve his motivation.

He thought back to the incident in the water and the vision of the golden owl, when the old man inside Blackskull Mountain flooded his thoughts. The old man's words reverberated in his ears.

"Don't be foolish Jimmy, that's not how this works; you have been done a great wrong. Your father wasn't killed by the Gatekeeper; it was someone even closer to your heart ...."

What did he mean by that? Who? *No! He was trying to trick me.*

The words continued. *"... I loved that world, the people, my family, and the thought of Tyranacus destroying it sent me crazy."*

"I can't bear the thought of destroying this world, but I will do it if that is what it takes," whispered Jimmy out loud. "There must be some other way that it can be healed without first destroying it ... And what about Talula wanting to destroy the world and then kill the Elders? This must be a nightmare; there's no way for me to win."

You must search out Higuain, the words flashed through his mind again followed by the warm sweet jasmine fragrance, which wrapped around Jimmy. He was too weak to resist and drifted off to sleep.

Jimmy was wakened by the sound of something scraping on the mirror. He opened his eyes, but saw nothing, nobody was there. Jimmy nestled back into his pillow and got comfortable once again until something screeched again. Jimmy sprang from his bed and ran to the mirror but instead of his reflection, he saw an image of his father. Jimmy pressed his palm onto the glass, closing his eyes and remembering.

Suddenly, a hand grabbed his wrist and before he had time to react he was dragged through the mirror. Jimmy landed on his knees. Scrambled to his feet he saw him ... his father. The last time he had seen him he was as an apparition made of water. This time he was made up of millions of tiny pieces of glass with thousands of rainbow coloured lights reflecting off his smooth crystal body.

"Jimmy, I don't have long. Argon told you the truth. You must find Higuain and help them. It is our only chance. Be careful, the Crinder is searching for you. He is trying to destroy you …'

Jimmy woke from his dream and saw that he was still in his bed. Dripping in sweat he patted his body making sure it was still there. He walked to the mirror. Only his tired, weary face looked back, no matter how hard and long he stared.

Grabbing his cloak and ruffling his tuft of ginger hair, he opened the bedroom door and walked onto the landing. Looking left, then right, he noticed that his room was the only one along the corridor. He walked to the left, running his hand over the cold bumps of the wall until he reached a dead end.

He'd barely taken five steps. Jimmy felt all over the wall and hit it with his fist, but it was firm, made of solid brick.

Jimmy turned to go back to his room, trying to work out how he would leave this tiny chamber when the ceiling started to wobble. A worn, dusty brown leather book fell through the ceiling and landed on the floor in front of him. A cloud of dust mushroomed into the air. He bent down and picked up the heavy book and blew the remaining dust off the cover. As his breath touched the ancient book, it sizzled in his hand and shrank down to a quarter of its size, about an inch thick.

Jimmy unclipped the latch on the side and saw a shimmering black digital tablet. The tablet came alive. A small icon appeared on the screen, 'The Door Application.'

Jimmy stared, puzzled. *What now?* The icon throbbed. He pressed the button and the page flickered blue. Letters appeared as though being typed onto the virtual paper by an invisible hand.

Instructions.

This is the application of doors created for Sepura Castle.

The application will reveal which doors you, as a student may enter, what teacher presides within the room and the lessons they teach.

The application will also reveal which doors or rooms are currently vacant and will direct you, via our tracking system, to every person's location within the grounds. Individuals are traced and updated via particles in their breath. Each time a person takes a breath of air the system is updated.

All you have to do is ask and all will be revealed. Use the application wisely and it will become a fantastic study aid.

For ease of use, the owner should use the 'minimise application' to shrink the tablet, enabling it to fit into the smallest of pockets.

Yours,

The Librarian.

A second application appeared on the screen with a *ping*, entitled 'Tracking App.'

Jimmy paused for a moment, checked up and down the corridor before he pressed the button and asked, "Where is Talula?"

The application buzzed under his finger and flicked though virtual data stopping on a blank double-page. An image of Talula in her room appeared on the left-hand side. She was pacing around her room. On the right-hand side, words appeared:

"Talula Airheart, room five. This is situated on the floor above your present location."

Jimmy pressed the button again and asked about the first room he'd seen when he first arrived in the castle, the room with the diamond window that contained the screaming face.

Once again, the application loaded and rifled through the data. It stopped. An image of the screaming face appeared on the page. The details gradually became clearer, revealing a man draped in a dusty brown coat, standing in a classroom in front of a chalk-covered blackboard.

Professor Lorda, master of Mythical Creatures and Legend. For transportation to the door, merely focus and think about the room.

The picture and words disappeared replaced by a message. 'You do not have access to these lessons!' The application crashed, and a red warning flashed.

Jimmy concentrated on the mysterious door for a few seconds and the carpet liquefied below his feet and he fell through the floor. Instantly he was forced back upward like a spring and landed on his feet, not outside his bedroom, but in the foyer of the castle.

Rubbing his chin in surprise, he pushed the button again, "Show me the location of everyone inside the castle."

The tablet growled and groaned, pulling away from Jimmy's hands and fell to the ground, the metal casing clanking on the marble floor. The application opened into 'Apocalyptic Maps', and hundreds of tiny blue pinpoint markers shuffled around the page

The names darted around the virtual map and Jimmy placed his index finger on the screen, dragging it across the glass. More markers came into view. He saw Talula's name, Percy's, Majordomo, Lorda … but there was a name walking about that Jimmy hadn't expected to see on there.

"Crinder!" He shouted the name his father had warned him about. "Show me Crinder, where is Crinder!" He pushed the name above the pinpoint marker.

The marker turned blood red and the processing wheel appeared in the corner. After only a few moments, writing appeared.

"There is no such person, apparition or spirit within the castle grounds."

The application returned to the front screen once again.

"But I saw the name Crinder," said Jimmy, puzzled. "I definitely saw the name on the map. It looked like it was near a tall wooden tower."

Percy, Harry and Talula shot up through the floor, startling Jimmy. All four of them now stood in the Grand Hall entrance.

"This place is amazing!" shouted Talula. "I looked out my room window and the gardens are exquisite. There is every kind and colour of flower and all manner of creatures and insects buzzing around. I also noticed a wooden bell tower right at the bottom. It was a little unusual. It was surrounded by dead flowers and covered in moss. It didn't seem to fit in with the garden at all. What do you have there?" she asked, staring at the tablet in Jimmy's hands.

"Urm, just an old book I, um, found on the floor." He tapped the minimize button and the hard metal casing folded in on itself until it was a quarter of the size. Jimmy shoved the miniature tablet into his pocket then turned to the group.

Percy opened his mouth to speak, but a wheezing breath startled them. Jimmy turned around and saw the butler standing behind them.

"I trust you enjoyed your rest period and refreshment? I am glad you are enjoying the sights, Lady Talula; especially the Old Bell Tower. That bell would ring twice a day, signalling sunrise and sunset, but suddenly—exactly one hundred years ago—it just stopped. I've been up there a few times, but I cannot figure out what happened. Come, I have someone for you to meet."

CHAPTER 5

Talula, Harry, Percy and Jimmy followed Majordomo towards an ornate wooden door covered in thick cobwebs. Harry elbowed the others out of the way and brushed away the cobwebs before trying force the door open. The grating of the hinges reverberated throughout the room. With one last shove he pushed the heavy door all the way open and it crashed into the wall.

The room rumbled as though a wild hurricane was approaching and before Harry had time to react a hundred books fell like rain from high above him sending him crashing to floor. Once the plume of dust that enveloped them had settled, all they could see were Harry's arms and head poking out from a pyramid of old books.

The others laughed as they stepped into the poorly lit, damp room. Jimmy shifted the books off Harry and helped him up. Jimmy heard footsteps behind him and barely had time to move out of the way as a creature burst through the dust. Jimmy stepped backwards, tripping over the pile of books and he too clattered to the ground.

The creature screamed, "My books, my books, be careful of my books. They are irreplaceable! Move away, move away!"

The creature approached, grabbing as many books as it could before delicately replacing them on the nearby shelves.

The children stared in amazement. Harry pulled himself free and rubbed his head, running his fingers over a swollen, painful-looking bump. He stopped dead when he saw the creature.

The creature had short, brown bobbed hair and was covered from head to toe with at least a thousand eyes. Harry stared at the largest three on the front of its face but as it blinked seven smaller eyes sprouting like antennas from the top of her head. The creature staggered about, using a thin piece of wood as a walking stick. It blinked all its eyes in one motion at the children then, banging the stick on the floor, made its way towards an old wooden counter.

"This is the Librarian, Madam Shrill," wheezed the butler. "She will assist you." Then he turned and clanked away down the corridor.

Not knowing what else to do, the children went to the desk. Madam Shrill was facing them and had a filing cabinet drawer open to her left. Her hand was rifling through some index cards. She stopped and pulled out some paperwork and Jimmy was amazed to see five blinking eyes – one on the end of each of her fingers.

The Librarian dropped the brown folder onto the desk, opened it and revealed black and white pictures of four young children.

"Ah, you have finally arrived," she said. 'You don't look anything like the last four. Never mind, I'm sure you will do fine. I am the Librarian, Madam Shrill. I was one of the first species on this world, in the … how do you say ... the testing phase, but I had too many faults. The Elders decided I would be kept and that this would be my role."

She turned and took a book from the shelf above her. A giant watering eye stared at the group from the middle of her spine. The Librarian dropped the book on the table and wiped the cobwebs off the front. Jimmy read the title:

The Life of Jimmy Damien Threepwood

Turning her many eyes towards Jimmy, Madam Shrill smiled and beckoned with her head for him to have a look.

Jimmy opened the back of the book. There it was, beautiful detailed images of him being dragged off the bridge into the black sea that surrounded Sepura Castle. Madam Shrill flicked through the pages and Jimmy caught glimpses of his journey with Talula in Frank the Frog, and the image of him thrusting his hand for the first time into the Elksidian Forest fire. At the very beginning of the book was his birth.

Jimmy stared at the Librarian in wonder.

"I have them for all of you. Your lives. I've been reading about you for years. But enough of that. There will be plenty of time later. Now, I have a pile of books for you to get you started on your studies. First you must receive your library cards. Pull up your sleeves and place your right wrists on the table."

The group did as they were told, holding their hands out, ready to receive the cards. Madam Shrill rifled under the desk and reappeared holding a giant metal stapler with two spikes poking out of the end like viper fangs. Before the children had time to move Madam Shrill stapled each wrist, "One, two, three, four, done."

Percy stepped back sucking in air through his teeth. Jimmy saw a small blob of blood and two small puncture wounds on his wrist. Between the holes were thin black bars and numbers.

"There you go. Now you have your barcodes inserted, any books you loan can be recorded, and I will know where to come to find them … if they are late! Come along and collect your books. I am centuries old … not as young as I used to be."

Percy and Harry walked around the desk and started rummaging through the piles.

"Ma'am?" asked Jimmy. "Have you heard of someone called Crinder?"

The Librarian sent books crashing to the floor and her lower lip quivered. "How did you hear that name? Who have you been speaking to? Never speak that name again. He is dead … died a long time ago."

Jimmy did not see what happened next.

*   *   *

A wave of dread poured over Talula. She stumbled and grabbed onto the wooden desk out of view of Jimmy and Madame Shrill, who were in deep conversation. Her vision faltered, and she felt sharp pains in her right hand. Her vision went hazy and she watched in horror as her right hand morphed into a hairy claw. Dirty yellow and brown nails burst out the tops of her fingers. Her eyes turned bright green, her pupils narrowed and became slits, like the eyes of a venomous snake. A voice sounded in her mind: "Killllll, Killllll, Killllll them!"

With her hand shaking, her nails dug into the soft wood of the desk, leaving deep scratches.

"Talula!" asked Jimmy, "Are you okay? You were making strange noises."

Talula shook her head and came out of the nightmarish daydream. Trying desperately to maintain her composure and show no sign of weakness to the others, she walked past Jimmy and went to collect her books, but the image of a giant bat like creature, with claws digging into her shoulders carrying her into the darkness, lingered.

*   *   *

Jimmy gave Talula an odd look then turned his attention back to the Librarian.

"Thank you for the Tablet, I've found out some useful things."

Surprised the Librarian stared at him. "Tablet? There is no such thing here. I don't dare embrace technology. I only have books and my books are precious, it's very rare I loan a book to anyone. Which one do you have?"

Jimmy reached into his cloak pocket and pulled out the miniature tablet.

"The Book of Doors!" gasped the elderly lady. "I haven't seen that book in nearly two thousand years, where did you get it?" Perplexed, the lady spoke again. "It's amazing that it is no longer a book. It has transformed to suit the needs of its owner. May I see it?"

Jimmy thrust it back into his cloak. "I found it near my room. I'll keep it safe for now and return it to you safely once I am done."

Jimmy grabbed his books and walked out of the library. He could see that there was something wrong with Talula, she was very quiet and distant, but she knew where he was if she needed to talk.

*　　　*　　　*

As the heavy library door slammed shut a gust of air extinguished one of the lamps on the desk. A shrill cry echoed high in the air and a shadow darted above the tall wooden book shelves. The Librarian glanced at the desk and saw the claw marks where Talula had been. She exhaled, tapping the five eyes on the ends of her fingers on the desk, deep in thought.

CHAPTER 6

L ate at night, shrouded in darkness, Jimmy switched on the tablet. He used his powers to produce a small green flame in his hands so he could see, and tapped The Door Application.

"Where is the Librarian?" he asked. The application flipped through the virtual pages and then stopped, showing him an image of the Librarian fast asleep in a room many floors away from the library.

"Show me everyone in the castle," he asked. The image of the castle spread across the screen. Jimmy couldn't see the name 'Crinder' anywhere. He checked on Talula and saw her in her bed, sweating and mumbling to herself. Something had happened to her today and it was clearly still affecting her. She hadn't spoken much and had been jumpy ever since they met Madam Shrill in the library.

He climbed out of his bed, opened the door and thought about the library. He was sucked into the carpet and found himself there seconds later.

As quietly as he could, Jimmy thrust open the giant door and ignited a second green flame to light the two candles on the desk. The sliver of light was enough for him to see the towering bookshelves. Rain was beating heavily on the domed glass skylight. He looked up and saw the cloud-covered moon staring back at him. Something moved in the top corner of the grand room. Startled, he raised his flaming hand and his eyes darted in every direction, but it was just shadows playing tricks on his mind.

As he moved along the bookshelves, Jimmy ran his finger over each of the ancient, dusty covers. They were arranged in perfect order but didn't contain what he was looking for.

Walking along the far wall, he rubbed the fingers of his left hand against the cold, rough stone. He stopped in front of a small indentation in the wall and turned to his right, staring at the letters on the next shelf. A bolt of lightning slashed through the night sky, illuminating the room for a split-second. Within the flash of light, a snarling, fang-toothed face appeared, hiding—pressed into the stone alcove behind Jimmy, its giant claws ready to strike as saliva dripped from its mouth.

Jimmy turned, thrusting his flame into the opening, but there was nothing there.

He turned his attention back to the bookshelf and spotted what he was looking for. He reached out to take it, but two shelves in front of him he saw a book fall to the floor with a crash. Apprehensive, he approached the book and peered at the title.

The Chiroptera Charmer

Jimmy bent down to pick it up. A high-pitched snarl came from the shadows. Jimmy grabbed the book, ran to the other shelf to take the item he came for and ran out of the entrance, closing the door tightly behind him.

The desk lights flickered out, casting the room into darkness except for a flashing light on a box near the door:

Barcode Scanner

*　　*　　*

A lone, cloaked female walked briskly through the narrow alleyway. Glancing upward, she saw the street sign declaring 'Black Friars Alley,' high on the white stone wall. Higuain had no idea why she had come to this alley of small, quaint, pleasant shops. For the past few nights she had found it very difficult to sleep as words kept reverberating around her mind in a distant, yet familiar voice, which wasn't her own.

"2PM be at Black Friars Alley ..."

Keeping her hood pulled over her head, she walked past the final shop and through an archway with a metal post in the middle to prevent vehicles driving any further. She was surprised when she saw that the top of the post was decorated with a metal brown owl.

She walked through the archway into a church courtyard and a breath of cold, fresh air swirled around her. The bells of the giant clock tower in the village rang twice, confirming the hour. As the path ahead opened, there lurking in the shadows, stood a young boy draped in long black robes shrouded in a mysterious blue aura. The boy pulled back his hood, revealing a tuft of ginger hair. He stared at Higuain. It was Jimmy.

Fear pulsated through her body. She checked left then right, "This a trap!?" she asked frantically and raised her hands, ready to strike. "You! I know what you are, demon. Where are your treacherous companions?"

A small spark appeared in the palm of her hands, ready to unleash a series of attacks. Her eyes darted around, searching for an exit.

"Wait!" shouted Jimmy. "There is no one else, it's just me. I mean you no harm. A voice ... a voice in my dreams asked me to meet you here."

He stepped onto the dusty gravel path and held his hands out in front of him. "I dreamt of an owl."

Higuain gasped. "Argon." *It was his voice, the voice that summoned me here,* she realised.

"Yes, Argon. I've already met him," said Jimmy. "We met whilst I searched for the Amulet of Trident. He told me what happened all those years ago. He told me how you all formed an army of light and tried to destroy Tyranacus ... how you failed."

"Then he also told you that he had waited for over two millennia until you four were born?" snarled Higuain. "He survived all this time - through an apocalypse - to save this world and stop it being destroyed again. He kept his army and his friends safe and I will protect him."

Jimmy remembered the old man Argon, and how he could barely raise his head to look at him.

"When I met him he was frail, he told me I was different from the others, he said he could see good in me ... that I was like him."

"You are nothing like him! You are monsters. Argon is old and weak; I don't know how long he will survive. But I will find a way to help him." Higuain turned and began walking away.

"Wait," shouted Jimmy, scrabbling inside his cloak. He pulled out a rolled-up scroll secured with a length of purple ribbon.

Uneasily, Higuain approached and snatched the fragile paper-cylinder from his grasp. She pulled off the ribbon, opened the scroll and her eyes scanned the ancient text.

Jimmy spoke again. "I don't know what that is, but in my dream Argon told me to bring it to you."

A smile spread across Higuain's face. She read from the page in a whisper.

"The scroll of the Granite Fairies. The Granite Fairies are guardians of the Palletine flower and are the only creatures that know the location of the last seed. I must return to the others. We have found what we have been looking for."

Full of excitement Higuain re-rolled the pages and pushed them into her sleeve. She smiled at Jimmy. "Perhaps he did see something in you after all," she said. Then she turned and ran away through the arch.

Jimmy reached into another pocket and pulled out a crumpled piece of paper. Staring at it, he had no idea what was so important about the scroll, but he knew that it was a map. He had made a copy for himself.

With a puff of purple smoke, Jimmy transformed into a majestic green phoenix and flew off into the sunlight.

CHAPTER 7

Jimmy burst through the open stained-glass windows, morphing mid-flight into his human form. A sliver of green fire dropped from his arm and began to burn on the soft carpet floor. He stamped his foot on the flame, extinguishing it. Then he sat at his desk and opened one of his study books.

Before he had chance to read one word, an ear-splitting alarm sounded. A public-address system screamed outside his room.

"TIME FOR YOUR FIRST LESSON! YOUR FIRST LESSON WILL BEGIN SHORTLY! PLEASE PREPARE!"

Jimmy didn't have time to react. His eyes glazed over, and an invisible force seized control of his body, sucking him through the floor. His body was frozen, and in front of him he saw a grand black door with a purple, pulsating, diamond at shoulder level. Jimmy was dragged through the trembling vortex into a blinding blue light.

He was pushed out the other side, a wave of nausea flooding his disorientated body. He was on a level he had not yet discovered. Holding his left hand over his mouth to prevent himself being sick, Jimmy glanced up. A giant round Christmas cake grabbed him and started shaking his right hand, speaking to him in a high-pitched voice.

"Jimmy Threepwood, at last we meet, so good to meet you at last, I am Professor Arual and I am the teacher of re-animation, a very useful lesson that will serve you well in the future. Please, take your seat."

Jimmy's head was pounding. *Does she ever stop to take a breath?* he thought. *Is the whole lesson going to be like this?*

As the haze lifted and his blurred vision corrected, he had a proper look at Professor Arual. She was completely round; wearing a chestnut brown cloak, Christmas green trousers and a white lace garment around her neck. She also wore a hat with a green flower, and bright pink lipstick. She hiccupped, once, twice before shooing Jimmy to his seat.

She's probably got hiccups through lack of oxygen after speaking for so long, thought Jimmy. He smiled to himself before walking to his seat.

Jimmy was a little surprised to see that his three companions were already seated at individual wooden desks. As he sat down behind Talula, she turned and smiled at him. Jimmy felt warmth whenever he saw Talula. Somehow, she always brightened up his day. *I don't know what I would do without her*, he thought.

Jimmy glanced around the room. There was a giant chalk board and Professor Arual sat in front of the class, perched on her grand wooden desk. Jimmy studied the classroom door, especially the small wobbling purple shape he had been sucked through. Adjusting his eyes, he noticed the air had a strange purple tint as though they were still inside the vortex.

Professor Arual sprang to her feet.

"Right! Time to begin (*hiccup*). Percy Timmins, come to my desk please, I will teach you all about the mysterious art of Re-animation (*Hiccup*)."

Percy got up and approached the desk. Professor Arual picked up an old shoe box and asked Percy to hold out his hands palms-up. Percy did so, cringing slightly. Professor Arual flipped off the lid and turned the box upside down. A human hand dropped into Percy's outstretched palm. It was a dirty green and completely lifeless. Percy flinched and scrunched up his face. A foul stench filled the room.

Jimmy saw Talula pull a sour expression as the smell reached her as she pulled her cloak over her mouth and nose.

"Now, my students," the teacher said, taking a piece of chalk and scribbling large letters on the board.

"Focus. Wave. Chant. That's the secret." Professor Arual dropped the chalk, which broke as it hit the floor. She pulled a wand that resembled a twig from a tree, out of a drawer.

"Abbbberrrennntoo," She waved her hand like she was directing an orchestra.

With a gentle crackle of bone and gristle, the dead hand jumped upright onto the tips of its fingers and darted along the table, jumping high off the end and crashing into a wastepaper bin near the door. The hand stood back up, shook itself, then scurried around the room again and under the feet of the seated children. Talula screamed and jumped up on to her chair.

The hand pulled itself up onto the window ledge, unlatched the painted-frame, pushed open the window and fell into the unknown. Percy, Harry and Jimmy ran to the window to see where it was, but it had disappeared.

"Quickly, children!" the teacher shouted, "Your turn. Talula, please get down."

The boys returned to their seats. A hiccupping Professor Arual placed four closed shoeboxes on their desks. Using her wand to flick off the lids, she told the group to turn their boxes over.

Talula sat down as Percy turned his box over and a dead toad splattered onto his desk. Brown liquid dripped onto the floor. A fly fell onto Jimmy's desk, but nothing fell out of

Harry's. Harry shook it and a spider unravelled from a web and dropped to the floor.

Talula pushed her box away from her and refused to turn it over. Her expression told Jimmy that the thought of it turned her stomach. The boys prodded their creatures with their fingers, and Talula eventually turned her box over. Out fell a small furry bat which landed on its back legs and stared at her.

*   *   *

Talula's eyes suddenly felt heavy and her breathing became shallow. She was overcome with warmth and dreamt of being carried away into the horizon by a giant bat... but she wasn't afraid, she wanted to be taken.

"Killllll thhhemmmm, Killl themmmm allll!" shouted distant voice.

Talula screamed. The bat sprang into life and flew into the air and straight out of the open window.

The others turned to look as Professor Arual shouted,

"We have a live one! Don't let it get away!" but it was too late. 'Don't worry Talula, watch the others and you'll get the idea. Okay students, off you go."

Talula could feel her hands trembling. *Why do I keep having that same dream? I'm not scared of it. It feels like a place I want to be.*

Talula heard Jimmy shout "Abbbberrrennntoo."

The fly, followed by the spider and then the toad rose and darted around the classroom.

*   *   *

Hours passed, and night fell on the castle.

Jimmy was fast asleep in his bed. The moon cast a penetrating light through the small square window, throwing shadows in the room. He tossed and turned as images of his father flashed through his dreams.

Jimmy was awoken by the sound of his room door creaking. He held his breath and remained on his side, waiting silently for another sound, but nothing. As he pulled the covers over his shoulder and closed his eyes, he heard a gentle groaning breath. Jimmy sat up, and in the darkness he saw two piercing snake eyes.

A razor-sharp claw slashed through the shadows towards him. At the last possible second, he rolled out of the way, taking the covers with him. Scrambling backwards, he watched the claw slicing through the pillows casting a plume of feathers into the air. Jimmy's eyes adjusted, and he saw the heavy creature breathing puffs of air, blue in the moonlight. The beady snake eyes were attached to a furry head with two floppy, pointed ears. Jimmy's eyes focused on the sharp pointed teeth, which were dripping with drool. The creature pounced, claws first, slamming them through the wall causing fragments of brick to crumble to the floor.

Jimmy sprang to his feet as the creature produced an ear-piercing shriek and focused on him. It towered over Jimmy. Two twitching wings hung from its back, smooth and leathery. Small clawed feet dug into the carpet.

Jimmy tried to compose himself and managed to create a flicker of energy in his hand. With a snap of the wrist, a lightning bolt pulsated through the air, but the creature arched its body out of the way. The bolt collided with the castle wall and exploded, large grey blocks of rubble crashed to the ground, showering the room with dust and gravel.

The creature screamed once more. Jimmy covered his ears to stop his eardrums from bursting as he dropped to his knees in agony. He staggered to his feet again, but the creature increased its pitch, the sound throwing him through the air, and he clattered hard into the wall knocking the breath from his lungs. Clambering back to his feet, Jimmy could barely breathe.

The relentless creature sprang towards Jimmy once more and grabbed him by the throat, lifted him high in the air and slammed him once more into the wall. Jimmy kicked his legs and tried to fight off the creature, but he was becoming weaker and weaker.

Jimmy stared into the beady eyes of the creature and saw a slight movement. A person was trapped behind the black pupils. He used the last of his strength, grabbed the claw with his hands and somehow managed to detach it from his neck. He took a deep breath. He stared into his attacker's eyes again and to his amazement he saw Talula. It looked as though she was trapped in a room banging on an invisible door, trying to escape.

Words struggled from Jimmy's mouth. "Talula? What happened to you?" Jimmy created a small electrical current in his hand and shocked the beast in the arm forcing it to release its grip and step back.

"Talula!" Jimmy screamed, "It's me."

The creature lurched forward and once again grabbed Jimmy. Time stood still as the beast raised its powerful right claw high in the air and thrust it at Jimmy. Panic took hold, but he was defenceless. He couldn't hurt Talula.

The claw shredded the air, moving closer and closer to Jimmy, then without warning it changed direction and slammed into the stone wall gouging out a giant chunk. The creature released Jimmy and the other claw dived into the wall as well.

"Jimmy!" the beast screamed. "I don't know how long I can ...."

The beast let out a roar and slowly started shrinking, changing into the form of a small human female.

"Talula!" Jimmy shouted, and tried to catch her before she collapsed to the floor.

Talula was unconscious, yet breathing, but had singed clothing and burn marks on her right shoulder from his electric charge.

Wearily she opened her eyes. "I'm sorry, I don't know what happened."

CHAPTER 8

The following morning Jimmy and Talula were sucked out of their rooms and pushed through the floor at the same time. They bumped into each other on the wooden walkway in front of a black door.

Talula was racked with guilt about what had happened. *How could she have tried to hurt Jimmy* she thought, saddened. But to her it had been just a bizarre dream. She didn't know what she had done until she had woken up. Her memory was hazy, filled with fog but she remembered standing amongst the destruction in his bedroom as droplets of blood trickling down his neck from her vicious claws. There was an uncomfortable silence, but then she raised her eyes, speaking softly.

"Jimm ...."

"It's okay, Talula, you were asleep. I could see that. It wasn't you; there's no need to explain. We'll need to find Lyreco to tell him what happened. Let's find him after class to see if this has ever happened before. It may be linked to your powers."

Smiling, Talula knew Jimmy had forgiven her, but it didn't ease her pain. *What if I hurt my only friend again,* she thought. *What I did to his father was bad enough, but to attack him? I must find out what's happening to me.*

The door in front of them vibrated and they were sucked into the classroom.

*   *   *

The students quickly took their seats but were surprised that there was no teacher. They gazed at the chalk board and the wooden desk in front of it then started to talk to each other. After a few minutes a voice rang around the room.

"Students! I've been waiting for silence!" a voice screamed from the chalk board area.

The group stopped, puzzled because there was no one there.

Percy was just about to speak to Talula, when the teacher's desk began to shake, and two hands appeared, clasping the wooden surface. The chair behind it scraped across the floor and a small man climbed up and stood on the desk. *That man's only three-foot-tall,* thought Jimmy.

Using his right hand, the small man brushed the long, floppy brown cone-shaped hat off his head and the small golden bell on the end jingled. Adjusting his tanned woollen tunic, the little man jumped up and down on the desk as his face turned a funny colour red.

"Timmins! I told you all to be quiet. That means you too!"

Percy nodded and diverted his eyes to the floor.

The teacher stopped jumping, took a deep breath and whipped a small telescopic pointer from a pocket in his yellow tights.

"Now, children," he said adjusting his waistcoat again.

"My name is Professor Tinker and I will be your teacher in Demonic Anatomy and Contact with Ghoul Minions."

Harry leant towards Jimmy and sniggered, "Little Tinker."

Professor Tinker glared at Harry. Once again, his face turned red and he jumped up and down on the desk, which bowed under his weight. With a swish of his pointer Harry's seat morphed into a green slimy octopus that wrapped its tentacles around Harry's mouth and held his head in place facing the front of the class.

"Now that I have silence, I will continue with what I was saying. Ghoul Minions."

The teacher turned and tapped the chalk board three times and a large cloth unravelled from above to reveal the image of a human.

"You may or may not have noticed, but the skin on each of you is slowly changing to a tint of light blue. This, my students, is the result of you using your dark powers. This is causing your skin to decay. Very soon, if not treated, your skin will fall off and you will become a blue-skinned hovering ghoul," Professor Tinker gave an evil smile. "We don't want that to happen, do we? The only cure for this is the blood of a Velosaras found in a berry growing on the Palletine flower. The juice is more commonly referred to … as the Elixir of Light. The Palletine is a magical flower tended to by a mystical race called the Granite Fairies. They are the only ones who know the flower's location.

"A single drop of the blood will refresh your skin and return your youthful complexion. But to gain the ultimate surge of energy and set you on your way to unlimited power, you will need to drink all the fluid. This will help your cells regenerate after injury and allow you to sustain the greater creatures within the scrolls. But be warned, the journey to the Fairies is long and treacherous, filled with many dangers."

*　　　*　　　*

I need that flower, thought Jimmy. *Once I drink it all, I will be an even stronger match for the Gatekeeper, especially if it will help me heal quicker during battle. The quicker we find it, the better I will feel.* He clenched his fist, awash with anger.

*　　　*　　　*

"There is a scroll in the library which will tell you how to find the Fairies and then you are on your own. This will be your next quest, but first I have a job for you to do."

Jimmy's heart sank, and it felt like the thrumming wings of a caged bird. Realisation dawned on him; he had already found this map and given it to Higuain. The map was gone, and the professors and the Elders would know it was he who had given it to the Light Dwellers. His pulse raced. He scrabbled in his pockets for the copy he had made, praying it was good enough to find the Fairies.

Professor Tinker was just about to explain what he wanted the class to do when a paper bird flew through the purple diamond, glided silently though the air and nosedived hitting the teacher's boots.

The professor bent down and picked it up. He unravelled it, a sour expression spread across his face and he mumbled under his breath, "You try to teach and there's always an interruption. Threepwood!" he shouted. "Madam Shrill wants to see you in the Library. Off you go, don't keep her waiting."

*　　　*　　　*

Jimmy stepped quietly through the open library door. Madam Shrill was kneeling, attending to the books on the bottom shelf of the book case. An eye in the centre of her back blinked. She turned around and using her walking stick pulled herself to her feet.

"Ah, Jimmy, you got my message."

Jimmy smiled. *I guess it was always right what they say. Teachers do have eyes in the back of their heads.*

"So, Jimmy," she continued. "I understand it is nearly time for your quest to locate the Palletine flower. It's very funny, I've been looking through my back catalogue and I'm missing a book and a scroll. The one needed to find the hiding place of the Granite Fairies and another. A very unusual book. A book that has been lost for over two hundred years. What do you have to say, Jimmy?"

Jimmy's expression gave him away as he tried to avoid Madam Shrill's gaze.

"Don't forget Jimmy, your barcode implant tells me every book that enters and leaves this room." She raised her walking stick and pointed at two small flashing red lights near the door.

Madam Shrill went to her desk and leaned on it.

"You are just like him you know. Even down to the colour of your hair. He was so different from the others. He would come in here and we would spend hours reading together. I couldn't bear to see him hurt or this world destroyed again, so I helped him. I helped Argon find his army of Light Dwellers and even how and when to strike the mighty Tyranacus, but there were not enough of them.

"I've read about you for years in the marvel that is the 'The life of Jimmy Threepwood.' Such a sad story, but I must admit, I took a sneak peek at the ending." She thrust her many eyes close to Jimmy's face and tapped her nose with a bony finger.

"I trust you still have the map you drew from the original? You will need it, so the others never find out you gave it to Higuain. Go now Jimmy, go back to class."

Jimmy walked towards the door. Madam Shrill spoke quietly, then stopped. Jimmy turned back to face her.

"Jimmy, I don't know how you got hold of that Chiroptera Charmer book, but you must read it and get ready. You and your companions are in grave danger. Be careful."

CHAPTER 9

Higuain burst through the swinging doors of the Egyptian exhibit shouting, full of excitement, brandishing the rolled up ancient scroll with the map showing the way to the Granite Fairies. Falling to her knees next to the solid stone Eclipse Portal she ran her hand over the rough coldness and whispered.

"Argon, I have the scroll. We now have the first clue to finding the flower that will rejuvenate you and make you young again. I will return with the flower and we will be together. I promise."

Enthused, she got up and ran to her three companions, who had remained at the exhibit, showing them the scroll.

Dravid took the delicate brown tube and gently opened it. He scanned the page showing the location of a race thought extinct centuries ago. A smile crossed his face.

"The Mountains of Wrath. They have been hidden in the Mountains of Wrath. No wonder they've not been found, the place is an ice-covered death trap. If you believe the rumours, the snowy mountains are home to Azzbecks, white fur-covered savages that can tear a human in half with one strike of their claws.

"Look, before you even get to the mountains you cross the Slithering Swamps. I ... I don't like this." His voice lowered and turned fearful.

Higuain approached and snatched the scroll from his grasp.

"We have fought worse than Azzbecks and crossed greater perils than a swamp. We have been fortunate to find this map and we must succeed, we will succeed whatever the cost."

Stratos roared. He slung his axe over his shoulder.

"How did you come by the map, Higuain? You left without a word and suddenly you have the answer to all your prayers? I don't like this."

Higuain was hesitant; thinking about her next words carefully before she finally spoke.

"It was Argon. He spoke to me in a dream and told me I needed to be at a certain place at a certain time and I would find the answers I was looking for."

"Argon!" Stratos roared. "He is locked in an eclipse portal. How could he have spoken to you?"

"I don't know how he did it, Stratos, but he did. I have the map as proof. When we find the elixir and rejuvenate Argon, he will take over as the leader of the Light-Dwellers. Until then I am in charge and you will follow my orders. Both of you fetch your belongings and be sure to pack something warm. This is going to be a dangerous challenge and you will need all your strength."

*　　　*　　　*

After Jimmy's meeting with Madam Shrill, a thousand questions flooded his mind. *Did she really help Argon build the Light Dwellers? What would Lyreco and the Elders do if they found out? What is so special about this book?*

Throwing his robe and notes on the bed, he pulled out the chair and dropped the heavy book onto the desk. He stared at the cover and ran his fingers over the leather-bound surface.

The Chiroptera Charmer

Intrigued, Jimmy turned to the first page and was surprised to see a picture of a thin boy aged about twelve or thirteen with slick, gelled back hair parted on one side. A blue and black striped jumper and a purple-lined robe hung from his slim frame, which seemed to stir on the page.

The wind blew, and a small branch knocked on the outside of the bedroom window startling Jimmy, who was reading intently. Turning back to the page he was sure the boy had aged by ten years and his parted hair had grown longer. Clasped in his right hand was a long golden instrument that Jimmy surmised was a flute.

In front of Jimmy's eyes, the boy on the page grew older and older until he was a man, who stared back through evil eyes.

As the image aged into what Jimmy believed to be his forties, the man raised the flute to his mouth and as he played, black notes danced along the page shuffling towards the edge of the paper. Forcing their way through the page, the notes exploded to life. The melody filled the room, waltzing around Jimmy's head, caressing his ears. Jimmy was transfixed by the lulling music and he felt as though he was sitting in the warmest, most comfortable chair he had ever sat in.

The music suddenly stopped, and Jimmy woke from the dream. The image of the man had lowered the flute to his side and two bare, black trees had grown on either side of him, a thousand beady yellow eyes staring back intently.

A menacing smile grew across the image's face and strands of hair grew out of his body as though an artist was flicking paint with a delicate brush. The hair continued to grow, and the man shrivelled on the page. Its features became pig-like with fangs bursting out of his mouth.

Giant wings grew out of his back and his clothes tore as his calf muscles and forearms doubled in size.

With an aggressive gesture, the creature flicked his fingers, revealing strong furry claws with razor sharp nails at the tips.

The image snarled, raising his claws in anger as the winged creatures flew above the trees covering the top of the page. With a strike, the monstrosity slashed with his left claw and somehow tore through the page of the book leaving four nail marks before the paper returned to its original rough texture. Jimmy slammed the book shut. *Who or what was that?* Thought Jimmy. *That robe, it looked like mine ... or the ones I've seen before.*

The door burst open and in charged Talula. Her eyes were wide and focused as she checked the room.

"That music," she said, with a hint of panic in her voice. "Did you hear the music, Jimmy?" Her eyes wandered, scrutinising every corner.

"Music?" Jimmy replied. *How could she have heard that? It was very faint; I could barely hear it myself.*

Talula ran her fingers over the leather cover of the book on the desk.

Talula grabbed the book, pushed it off the table and it crashed into the wall. The book fell to the floor, opening on the two blank centre pages.

"No!" she screamed, "I won't do it!" She turned and ran into the corridor.

Jimmy looked around to see who she was talking to and ran into the corridor after her, but she was gone. Emotions overwhelmed Jimmy. All he wanted was to protect her and keep her safe. *What's happening to her?* Something was wrong with Talula and he had to find out what it was, and soon …

Jimmy went back to his room and heard the gentle patter of rain bouncing off his window. Outside he could see the dark, purple sky. A bolt of lightning tore through the air, illuminating the spindly Old Bell Tower. A feeling of imminent dread swirled in the pit of his stomach.

CHAPTER 10

The following morning, Lyreco was sitting in his room in a high corner of Sepura Castle, focusing on drawing power from the dark red crystal hanging around his neck. As his fingers rubbed the smooth glassy surface, his mind wandered to the flickering abomination that had clawed its way out of the black sea surrounding Sepura Castle. He focused, recalling how black shadow had slowly melted over its body, leaving a bearded man. Time can make people forget, but he would never forget that face or that day ....

* * *

Centuries earlier ...

The morning sun was intense. Lyreco wiped the beads of sweat from his brow and peered over at his brother, Hellsby, who was busy tightening the string on his wooden bow.

"Hellsby," Lyreco shouted, "We are prepared. The plan is in place and we strike tonight. I've spoken to my contact in the castle and I have acquired a master key to the locks."

"Good work, my brother," replied Hellsby. "At nightfall we shall sneak into the castle and be rich, rich beyond belief. King Randolf has far too much gold if he can give so much of it away to these pathetic villagers. I am sure they will survive even after we have helped ourselves." An evil smile spread across his bearded face.

"Tonight, my brother, the Dark Reefers will rise and become the greatest of all the thieves' guilds." Both men shouted in laughter. Their plan was ready to unfold.

*   *   *

Night fell upon the village, which was illuminated only by a few scattered torches. The flames flickered, creating plenty of shadows for the two thieves to hide.

"Hellsby, it's time to go."

Hellsby grabbed his bag, slid his sword into its leather holster and stepped out of the wooden shack. He pulled the door shut. Something nudged the back of his mind, giving a feeling of deja-vu and a flash of a distorted future event. He had an uneasy feeling that he would need to take his bow and plenty of arrows. The tips had been freshly dipped in Thormax, the most potent poison in the world; only found in rare pink mushrooms in one section of the forest. Hellsby collected his bow and strapped the arrows to his back. Having joined Lyreco, they set out into the night.

Hours passed. Helsby and Lyreco were running through the shroud of darkness. They pressed themselves into the castle wall and their dark shadows slipped into the blackness. Wiping the sweat from their heads, their hearts raced with adrenaline. The brothers pulled masks over their grubby faces and scurried along the wall like rats in the night. Patrolling high on the castle keep was a guard armed with a bow and a quiver of arrows. He peered into the darkness, unaware of the intruders.

The pair tiptoed along a gravelled path, covered in dirty, sparsely-sprinkled hay, down an embankment to a metal gate, which led to the dungeons.

Lyreco pulled a silver key from his pocket and slowly turned the lock until the barrel clicked. Checking over their shoulders to make sure they'd not been followed, they pushed open the gate. It squealed on its rusted-metal hinges and they held their breath before continuing.

They could hear one another but had to wait for their eyes to adjust.

"You took your time!" an angry voice said beside them.

Hellsby jumped and stepped back in fright. He stumbled into Lyreco and almost fell, his feet landing in a puddle of filthy water.

A torch illuminated an old face with leathery, wrinkled skin. The man lit a second torch, and passed it to Lyreco who held it high. The man's Centurion helmet and uniform became visible.

"Come on, this way, we have to be quick," said the Centurion. He turned and sloshed through the dirty sewer-water.

"This is your contact? A Centurion? How can we trust him?" asked Hellsby.

Lyreco lowered his voice to a whisper. "Do not worry Hellsby. I've taken care of everything."

The Centurion guard approached the dungeon door. The sounds of the weak prisoners inside were projected as moans of agony and hunger. Fumbling on his belt, the Centurion produced a large ringed holder and selected the master key. He put the key into the lock, the barrel dropped and with a creak the door opened.

"We muuuhhh …."

Before the guard had time to speak Lyreco thrust a dagger deep into his back. The guard staggered and dropped to his knees. With his final breath, the guard spoke. "We had a deal," he said, before falling—face first—into the dirt.

Hellsby laughed at his brother's actions. He bent down, thrust his hands into the dirty water and grabbed the key ring.

"We have the master key. We have access to the whole castle."

Lyreco smiled, "The treasure room is this way. Let's go."

After running through a maze of dark corridors, Lyreco skidded to a halt and searched his tunic pockets. He pulled out an old, torn map. His tongue poked out while he thought, and he ran his dirty, blackened finger over the paper.

"Here it is!" he shouted. "Quickly, pass me the key."

Lyreco put the key into the lock. He turned it with a click and the door swung open. They stepped through the door and were temporarily blinded by the intense reflections of the king's treasure. Slowly the pair entered the room and were amazed to see the sheer amount of gold and jewellery, which would soon be theirs. Lyreco's eyes were immediately draw to and mesmerised by the glowing intense-red of a stone set into a necklace that was locked in a glass case in the centre of the room. Lyreco was drawn to it and punched the case hard. The glass shattered, and the noise echoed around the room. He reached out and touched his fingers to the stone for the first time …. He could feel his heart ignite.

"Quickly!" Hellsby said, and he held out two woven sacks. Lyreco shook himself free from his trance and the pair filled the sacks with all manner of gold, as fast as they humanly could. They were surprised when the first rays of the morning sun shone through the window.

"The guards will be doing their rounds. We have taken too long. We must go now!" shouted Hellsby. He was frantic. He grabbed Lyreco's sleeve and hauled him out of the room.

The two shuffled along as swiftly as they could with the weight of the sacks digging into their shoulders. Hellsby kicked open the dungeon door and they ran back through the corridors until they saw daylight illuminating the exit.

Lyreco was unable to get the red stone out of his mind. All of a sudden, the anxiety drained from his body and nothing else mattered, nothing else but that stone. It was as though someone was influencing his mind.

"Wait!" shouted Lyreco. "The stone ... I've forgotten the stone ... I must go back!"

Before Hellsby could open his mouth, Lyreco dropped the heavy sack into the sludge and ran back the way he had come.

Minutes passed by when Hellsby's stomach turned to ice as the castle bell wailed throughout the grounds, followed by the sound of panicked loud voices and footsteps filling the air.

"A thief! We have captured a thief! To the king!"

Hellsby lowered his gaze and shook his head. "Fool! We had riches beyond belief, but he wanted more. He always wanted more."

Helsby closed the gate behind him and strode off into the morning sunshine.

*　　*　　*

Lyreco was dragged through the cobble-stone square. Battered and bruised, he used the last of his strength to raise his head to see the hundreds of town-folks gathered to watch. They were heckling and cheering to see the hanging of the man found guilty of stealing the king's treasure. Some of the crowd became angry, screaming for justice for their beloved king and throwing rotten fruit. It missed Lyreco but instead splashed on the market floor.

Lyreco was dragged up the wooden steps and a noose slipped over his head. His face froze in a glassy stare of horror and his body quivered with fear. Images of his friends, family, loved ones flashed in front of eyes. He tried to look away, but he was surrounded by angry faces, each one hurling abuse and chanting for his death.

Two bugles announced the king's entrance and music swelled as a brown-bearded man followed a procession of Centurions up the stone steps. The king sat down on a wooden throne with a clear view of the prisoner. His large red coat draped over his frame and his golden crown glistened in the afternoon sun.

The king rose from his seat and there was silence. Even the birds stopped squawking.

"My people, am I not a fair, honest and generous king?" he demanded.

The people roared, throwing their hands high in the air.

"However! This man before you, Lyreco Knightsbridge has chosen to take more! To steal from the royal vault. He tried to take your taxes; money to be spent on *your* food. But, he was caught by my Imperial Centurions and he will be used as an example to anyone wishing to steal from this kingdom."

King Randolf raised his right arm in salute and once again the crowd cheered their beloved king.

A bare-chested giant of a man, his face covered in a black iron mask, tramped up the steps. Each thud bringing Lyreco's life closer to the end.

Lyreco felt his throat tightening. He struggled for breath and couldn't swallow because his mouth was too dry. He wanted to vomit, but managed to hold it in.

The Hangman held the rope switch to release the mechanism and awaited King Randolf's final instruction.

The king held his arm up. Suddenly something fizzed over the Hangman's head. An arrow tore through the air, over the crowd and hit the king straight in the chest. The king's hand dropped slowly, a look of shock in his eyes.

It took a few seconds for the crowd to register what had happened, but as the king dropped to his knees, screams filled the air. A second arrow plunged into the hangman, then the guard at the bottom of the wooden steps.

Lyreco raised his head, looking directly into the sunlight, yet still able to make out his brother, Hellsby, on top of the castle wall.

"Go!" Hellsby screamed as he fired another arrow, hitting the next closest guard in the throat.

Lyreco wriggled free from the noose and jumped into the pandemonium below. Pushing through the crowd, he reached the gate under which Hellsby was standing; still launching a barrage of arrows.

Frantically, he staggered out of the gate and saw two horses which appeared to be waiting for him. He pulled himself up and looked over his shoulder to see his brother dive off the castle wall and land in a convenient pile of hay. Hellsby jumped onto his horse and they both escaped into woodland.

*　　　*　　　*

Hours passed, and the pair finally slowed down to rest.

Dismounting from their horses, Lyreco grabbed his brother and embraced him.

"You came back for me!"

"Yes," Hellsby said smiling, "you owe me one, although I did leave it to the last second for effect."

Lyreco held his head and inhaled a large breath of air.

"What did you do with the gold?"

Hellsby smiled again. "You are nearly executed, yet the first question is about the …"

As the last word had left his mouth, his attention was drawn to the sound of rustling leaves in the undergrowth behind them. The ground started to rumble, and a purple distortion appeared in the air in front of them. The vortex grew larger and larger before a black-cloaked figure glided through, holding a glistening, razor-sharp scythe. The portal snapped shut behind him. It was the Gatekeeper.

Hellsby drew his sword and charged toward the unearthly creature, swinging his blade and screaming. He swung down with his sword with all his power but in a flash the creature raised its own deadly weapon and sliced clean through Hellsby's blade. In the same motion, the deathly creature struck Hellsby in the stomach with a bony, decaying fist, sending him hurtling into a tree.

The creature snarled and faced Lyreco.

Lyreco pulled a small knife from his belt and flung it at the apparition like he had done so many times previously at different enemies This time however, the creature merely raised its left palm and the knife burst into flames.

Lyreco tried to run, but using an invisible grip the creature picked him up and slammed him onto the ground.

The creature glided to Hellsby who was semi-conscious at the foot the tree. He reached down and took Hellsby by the throat. With no effort at all, the creature lifted him high into the air, pinning him against the tree as if he weighed nothing. Hellsby struggled and kicked his legs but all to no avail.

A deep, deathly voice echoed throughout the forest.

"You dare take the life of someone not meant to die!? It is written that King Randolf would die in forty years and Lyreco Knightsbridge would die today. I don't know why you returned to save your brother, but I will take your soul as a consequence, to restore the balance ... that is ... unless your brother, Lyreco, volunteers to take your place and comes with me as was ordained."

Lyreco crawled along the dusty forest floor and gazed into the eyes of his terrified brother; the brother who had risked it all to rescue him.

Hellsby gave a last wheeze of breath. "Help me ..."

Lyreco turned and ran though the undergrowth as fast as he could. As he ran, he could hear the screams behind him.

*   *   *

The creature's hand emanated black and the flesh on Hellsby's neck started to wither and die. With a powerful thrust, the creature pulled a flickering shadow from within Hellsby's body. A vortex opened to consume it and the Gatekeeper cast Hellsby's soul through it.

The creature released its grip and the lifeless body collapsed to the floor. With a crackle, the Gatekeeper was gone.

*   *   *

Lyreco ran as far as he could until exhaustion made his muscles give way and he tripped over a log and fell to the floor. He tried in vain to get up, but he couldn't, and his vision started to fade.

A voice prompted him to open his eyes. Fear pulsed through his body, *the creature had found him*. But it wasn't the creature. Through his exhausted eyes, Lyreco saw a man draped in a flowing-white gown. The man had a brown moustache that curled at the ends. Lyreco could barely move.

"So, Lyreco. We meet at last." The man opened his gown and pulled out the gleaming red stone that had cost Hellsby his life.

"I am Lord Trident, one of the Elders who created this earth. We protect it from harm. You have met one of my companions; the Gatekeeper. He is here to keep the balance between life and death. From the moment I saw you I knew you were the snivelling coward I was looking for, a coward that would let his own brother die and be cast into an eternity of misery and suffering.

"I was the one who caused you both to deviate from your written paths. I made your brother bring the poisoned arrows; I made you return for this stone, resulting in your capture and it was I who made your brother return to save you."

"Why?" asked Lyreco.

"Because you are the perfect vessel for my plan. My body is becoming frail and weak, but I can sustain your human form for centuries. I intend to implant part of my soul in you so that you will become my minion and use the power I grant to train my forthcoming warriors. You will have your own thoughts and will, but I will control you."

Lord Trident breathed into the red crystal and a trail of orange dust filled the air. He approached Lyreco and placed the crystal around his neck.

"Rest now my servant, the end of this world is fast approaching."

CHAPTER 11

In the present …

Lyreco opened his eyes and studied the amulet that had graced his neck for centuries. He was awoken from his daydream by the rustle of bushes and the snapping of twigs in the distance. Peering out of the window across the wooden bridge he saw him; a ghostly figure stepping out of the forest. It stopped in plain view. A face he never thought he would see again

"Hellsby!" he whispered. "But how?"

The bearded man stared up at Lyreco before turning and disappearing back into the woods.

A wave of confusion and guilt flooded over Lyreco as he sprang from his chair and ran out of the room to give chase.

The tall forest trees blocked any daylight and cast shadows along the woodland floor. In the distance he could see Hellsby pausing, waiting for Lyreco to catch up and then darting off once again into the darkness. Lyreco panted heavily. The only thought he had was seeing his brother again, telling him he was sorry. It was the only thing that gave him the strength to continue.

Lyreco compelled his weary body through the undergrowth as branches scraped past his face. Dead leaves crunched under his feet and in the distance, Hellsby stopped. Lyreco staggered on, shouting, "Hellsby, wait!"

Stumbling with exhaustion, Lyreco stepped on a fallen branch and as he did, it rolled, causing him to lose his footing and slam to the ground. He caught his forehead on a loose stone and through dazed eyes saw his brother, showered in sunlight. Hellsby was beckoning him to continue.

Lyreco struggled to his feet and wiped the stinging gash on his forehead, wiping the blood into his tunic. The throbbing headache was intensified by the heat and bright light of the sun. He stepped into the clearing the students had used as a training arena only months before.

Holding his hand to his head to block out the light, Lyreco considered the circular area where the tree line had been cut back to make a ring to maximise space. He saw a fire roaring in the centre and the five tree stumps they had previously used as seats.

Hellsby stepped out of the shadows behind Lyreco.

"My brother," he said. "It is good to see you again after all these years."

Lyreco turned and dropped to his knees. Guilt flooded his body.

"Hellsby ... you are alive! I thought I lost you all those years ago. Where have you been?" Lyreco crawled to Hellsby's feet, stricken with the pain of past events.

"You had the chance to save me, brother, but you left me to die!" Lyreco could hear the centuries of rage and torment in Hellsby's voice.

"I am sorry. I was weak ... I was scared."

Hellsby smiled, and said, "and now it is your turn," before turning and walking slowly into the darkness of Elksidian Forest.

Tears of rejection trickled down Lyreco's bruised face. He held his hand out, begging for his lost brother to forgive him.

Lyreco tried to get to his feet, but the ground started to rumble. In front of him, a dark purple diamond formed. It produced a static charge and crackle in the air that pushed Lyreco's weak body backwards. Before Lyreco had time to react, the deathly Gatekeeper tore through the vortcx, wrapped his bony fingers tight around Lyreco's neck and lifted him into the air.

In a dark, unearthly voice, the repugnant creature spoke. "Lyreco, I've waited a long time for this moment. I thought it only fitting that I cast your brother out of my desolate prison to bring you here to me. The brother you let die in your place centuries ago."

The luscious grass in the area had withered, turning black as the dying trees slowly bent forward blocking out the morning sun and casting the training area into darkness.

Lyreco gasped for air but managed to produce some words.

"Gatekeeper, why are you doing this? Why now?"

The deathly creature laughed. "It was written that you would die centuries ago and I came to collect your soul, but someone ... some ... thing ... interfered. It altered your path.

"Your brother saved you and killed the king. Randolf was not due to die. The balance was wrong. As a result, the earth would have torn itself in half. To protect it, I took the life of the person who caused the anomaly in the first place; your brother."

Lyreco struggled for air and kicked his feet, but the Gatekeeper continued. "Then, you have the audacity to trick me. Me: The Keeper of Life and Death—into distracting Jimmy Threepwood while you blamed me for killing his father! Threepwood is but a bug to me; one I could crush in my fingers, but Bill Threepwood was not supposed to die. You took a life early and I've come to restore the balance once more."

With a flash of brilliant yellow light, Lyreco's right palm illuminated. He thrust his magic into the immortal's shoulder. With a roar of pain, the unearthly Elder dropped Lyreco and staggered backwards.

"So that is why you have come for me ..." Lyreco said. "... but things are different now. The last time we met I was but a mere mortal. Now *I* have the powers of an Elder!"

A shower of meteors burst from Lyreco's hands. They scorched the ground and engulfed The Gatekeeper in a cloud of thick black smoke and ash.

"This is Elksidian Forest! It has been enchanted by Lord Trident himself. Neither the students nor I can be harmed here," Lyreco said.

The cloud of smoke burst open and the Gatekeeper reappeared. His mouth opened with a snarl and a thousand black, flesh-eating beetles streamed out, latching onto Lyreco and tearing through his skin and clothes.

Screaming in pain, Lyreco doused himself in fire and the insects dropped to the floor.

"You are a fool, Lyreco! I am more powerful than anything on this earth. No spell can contain me."

Lyreco put his hands to his face, the intense pain causing his body to quiver. The beetles had ravaged his face tearing away his skin and leaving chunks where his bone was exposed.

Drawing his last ounce of strength, he reached over his left shoulder and pulled out a glowing V-shaped metal object.

With one final push he thrust it as hard as he could at his deathly opponent.

The Gatekeeper simply stepped out of the way and the weapon zipped past his head with a swish.

In response, the Gatekeeper opened his left palm and produced a whip made of solid metal chain, which pulsated with dancing sapphire flames. The chain extended, flicked and wrapped itself around Lyreco's body. He collapsed to his knees, wheezing as the chains tightened around his chest. Lyreco looked up just in time to see the enchanted V shaped boomerang he'd thrown returning on its path. It crashed into the back of the Gatekeeper's head, smashing a hole in his head and causing the hood to drop, revealing the brown, withering skull of the immortal. The Gatekeeper snarled as he reached to the back of his head and snapped off the shattered piece of skull, before discarding it on the floor.

The Gatekeeper's eyes glowed red and two thin beams of light streamed out and bored into Lyreco's skull. Lyreco hollered in pain. The Elder slowly opened his mouth again and hissed. A shower of white hot fire unleashed from the Gatekeeper's mouth encased Lyreco in a cocoon of lava stone. With one swift motion, the Gatekeeper lifted his scythe and smashed the stone to pieces. Satisfied, the Gatekeeper reached out one skeletal hand and snatched the flailing, shadowy soul.

With a roar of victory, The Gatekeeper forced open a void and stepped back into his unearthly prison ...

The pile of rubble crumbled and gently drifted away on the breeze. The trees and grass slowly rejuvenated. The red crystal necklace fell to the floor and the orange particles of Lord Trident's breath soaked into the ground.

CHAPTER 12

Beads of perspiration trickled down Stratos's forehead as the intense morning sun burned the nape of his neck. With each step his shield became heavier and heavier.

In the distance a cluster of houses came into view at the end of the dusty, gravel path they were following.

As they approached, they saw the eerie, untouched entrance to a ghost town that once looked to be a prosperous family village. A spindly wooden frame towered high above the entrance. An old piece of tattered wood swung on its chains creaking in the quiet morning breeze. Surrounding the town was a sparsely-filled hedgerow. Battered by the elements, the hedgerow was home to all manner of lifeless flowers and animal carcases. Flies circled it like starving buzzards in a blazing desert.

"Welcome to Pickington, population 502," said Dravid tilting his head to read the sign.

The entrance to the village was marked by a statue of a woman. She was surrounded by a ring of stone filled with glistening clear water. The statue grumbled, and a stream of water spurted from the jets in her hands and mouth, churning up the water below.

Stratos pushed past his companions and went to the water.

"At last!" he roared, and he crouched down cupping his giant hands. He splashed the cooling water over his face and hot neck, before slurping it from his palms.

The journey and heat had taken its toll on all of the weary travellers. Dravid and Higuain looked thirsty too, but as they approached the fountain, Stratos saw a flicker of movement out of the corner of his eye.

"Did you see that?" asked Higuain. Stratos was still engrossed in the fountain but Dravid stepped forward,

"Yes. You there, we have seen you. Show yourself."

Silence ...

Higuain shouted this time. "Show yourself, we are armed!"

There was a moment's pause followed by a dry rasping cough. A small, raven-haired girl wearing a long dirty white gown staggered toward them. She scuffed her feet in the dirt, let out a deep sigh and extended her arm toward Dravid.

"No ..." breathed the girl, before collapsing to the floor.

Dravid rushed to her side, scooping her into his arms and holding her head. Her skin was green and oily. The soft area around her lips and eyes was white and powdery. The girl, who couldn't have been more than six, was still breathing, but it was shallow and raspy.

In the distance, on the far side of the town, Dravid spotted a female waving her arms, trying to gain their attention. She appeared fragile and was using the wooden frame of the house to support her feeble body.

Dravid scooped up the child and walked toward the woman, calling Stratos to follow. The centre of the town was completely empty. Despite the sweltering day there were no children playing, people talking or even dogs running around.

"What has happened here?" asked Higuain, trying to look through curtains and windows for any sign of life. Every other window was boarded up and smeared in graffiti and paint.

Wooden doors were hanging off their hinges and piles of rubbish were strewn across the street.

Using his foot to push aside a broken wooden cart Stratos's mind wandered to the last time they had walked through this town centuries ago. The screams of laughter and children playing on the road ghosted around what the previously-bustling market town had become.

On reaching the woman, Dravid immediately realised that she was weak and malnourished. Her dry cracked lips formed a soundless 'thank you' as she stumbled, sliding down the side of the house. Higuain rushed forward and lifted her to her feet before assisting her into the house. Dravid had already entered and was placing the fallen child on a mattress in the living room. The smell of the house struck Higuain like a force and she covered her nose from the foul, pungent swamp smell floating in the air. Higuain stared at Dravid and nodded to the hundreds of blowflies buzzing round the room.

Higuain sat the female in a chair and tapped Dravid's side to get his attention again when she noticed a male slumped unconscious on a second mattress in the corner of the room.

The female murmured, "It will be okay, he will be coming today … we just need the medicine." Her eyes became heavy and her head rocked back against the chair.

"Do you know what's wrong with them?" asked Higuain.

Dravid approached and used his fingers to open her eyelids. Her pupils were grey and lifeless. "No, I've never seen this type of disease. It's as though they are suffering from a virus or even a plague of some kind."

"What do you think she meant by 'he' is coming with medicine?"

Dravid used the back of his hands to test the female's temperature. "She is burning up. She will need help and soon.

I will do what I can to help her, but I must treat the girl first. I will keep her comfortable until the person she talks of arrives."

The image of Argon's frail body collapsing before her flashed through Higuain's mind and she felt crushing pain in her chest, knowing that his life was ticking away.

"What about Argon?"

"Higuain," Dravid snapped, "I cannot leave these people. They are mortally ill. Argon would not want me to leave them. Once we have helped them we can continue on our quest."

Guilt rumbled in her stomach and she wiped her face. "Of course. I'm ... I'm sorry, I didn't mean that. We must help these people. Do you think the other people in the town are the same?"

"I don't know," whispered Dravid, "I hope not, I sincerely hope not."

Hours passed by as Higuain placed towel after towel drenched in chilly water onto the woman's head. Dravid was doing tests on the young girl until he shouted: "The girl is ready. Her temperature has dropped, and she is coming around."

He used his right hand to support her head and focused. His eyes turned white and a clear blue, a wobbling gel substance trickled along his veins, through the young girl's head and into her body.

The girl started to shake, her legs twitched, then stopped, and she remained still.

Dravid reacted, scrunching his face up in pain. The blue fluid faded and turned a thick, dirty green-black. It was like poison and it drained from the young girl's body into his.

The substance slowly covered his arm, biting and drawing the nutrients from his blood as it filtered through his body, climbing his neck and covering his face. Dravid screamed and exhaled. The crystallised poisonous green gas left his mouth evaporating into the air and in an instant, it was over. Dravid collapsed to the floor breathing deeply as the colour slowly returned to the young girl. The white powder around her lips and eyes returned to normal.

Higuain helped the weary Dravid from the floor. He stood catching his breath while his body returned to normal.

"I will need to rest for a few hours before I can help the mother. That is a potent poison. It's not a virus,"

Dravid rested and the stale, quiet air was filled by deep moans coming from Stratos who was bent over clutching his stomach.

"Urrgh, I don't feel too good," he grumbled.

"Stop complaining," snapped Higuain. 'Once we help this village we can ..."

She was stopped mid-sentence by a catchy jingle dancing through the silent air of the town.

CHAPTER 13

Higuain opened the curtains and tried to see the source of the music. It reminded her of the tune she had heard many years ago played from loudspeakers on ice cream vans.

In the distance a cloud of dust followed a bright blue stage coach with a chorus blasting from its horns. The brightly coloured carriage was being pulled by four giant black hogs that skidded to a halt opposite Higuain's window.

Sitting high above the hogs was a thin man with weasel features who sniffed the air as he adjusted the purple pointy hat with a long yellow feather. He carefully positioned the hat so that it was slanted on the side of his head.

Jumping from his seat, he landed on the dusty ground and Higuain saw a luscious purple silk suit and yellow suede shoes. He grasped a long cane in his right hand.

With a gesture of confidence, he flung both arms high above his head as though he was king of the world. The moment his hands reached the summit two loud shots were fired from pipes on the roof of the carriage causing Higuain to flinch. Orange smoke and confetti filled the air.

"Ladies and Gentlemen," the brightly-dressed man squeaked. "Come and get your medicine! Come and get it now, before it's all gone."

With another self-assured gesture he banged the side of the carriage. Bold, colourful letters painted on the sides of the carriage, declared that it was 'Dr Vantargo's Fantilium.' On cue, the side panel dropped open, held by two firm chains on either side. It looked as though he had opened a shop in the middle of the street.

The strange orange gas filtered into the air, and into the house. Behind Higuain, the female and male's eyes opened, and they groaned like zombies. There was blackness behind their eyes and without acknowledging Dravid, they both slowly rose and staggered out into the street.

The other residents of the town were gathered in front of the portable shop-front. They started to groan and scrabble past each other, trying to get to their medicine.

"Ah, my friends, have no fear! I, Dr Vantargo have arrived to sell you my mysterious, magical, all-healing Fantilium potion. In but a few moments you will be fit and healthy and on top of the world once more."

The crowd were groaning like mindless zombies, rummaging through their bare pockets and pulling out the last of their coins. One by one they reached the window and bought the mysterious potion.

Higuain and Dravid walked out of the house and stood out of the way of the crowd, with their backs against the wall.

"Look at them," said Dravid, "they are like wild animals. I need to find out what this potion is."

Dr Vantargo raised his eyebrows and peered at the approaching man, clearly surprised to see that he was healthy. He tapped his fingers on the counter and a sinister smile spread across his face.

"My clients. It seems we have new guests to our town. Guests who have come to share your medicine."

Instantly the sound of groans spread through the air. The noise was so loud it sounded like a chorus of bees buzzing. In unison the townsfolk turned towards Dravid, rage on their faces. The medicine was all they had, the only thing that kept them alive, and they would protect it at all costs.

The townsfolk snarled, and saliva dripped from their mouths. Some raised pitchforks, others grabbed torches and set them alight.

Dravid quickly retreated and turned towards Higuain.

"Walk back slowly, Dravid. We can't harm them," said Higuain.

"It's the poison. It's taken over their minds like a parasite," said Dravid, moving carefully away.

"But!" the doctor shouted, and the horde of angry townsfolk turned back to him, "I've enough for everyone here today. Please come and collect your medicine and you will be well again."

On his command the community dropped their weapons and formed an orderly line. Dr Vantargo glanced at Higuain and Dravid and smiled.

The female that Higuain had helped into the house, used the last of her money to buy the medicine. Higuain watched as she popped off the corked lid and emptied the vial of glowing green fluid into her mouth.

Once the townsfolk had taken the vials Higuain and Dravid tried to walk through the group to speak to Dr Vantargo to find out what was going on. By the time the last person opened their bottle top Dr Vantargo was already perched atop the carriage. He whipped his giant hogs and they took off at a gallop. The doctor raised his bag of money high above his head and shouted: "I will see you all in two days for your next dose of Fan...til...ium!" He purred the word. The carriage roared past Higuain and in a flash, he was gone, the tracks of the carriage covered in a plume of dust.

Some of the townsfolk were staggering about, but most were on their knees, grumbling and rocking back and forth. Dravid saw the woman he had helped earlier. Her eyes were closed, and her head was drooping towards her chest. Her head then started to shake and Dravid ran toward her pushing past the others just in time to catch her before she fell. Cradling her in his arms he stared at her head and to his amazement a large bump appeared under the skin on her forehead and travelled quickly down her face. As it reached her oesophagus she choked, coughed and she exhaled a cloud of green dust, which drifted into the air and swirled around her body from head to toe before fading away.

With a giant breath the woman's eyes shot open. She pulled away and cowered from Dravid, like she had never seen him before.

"It's okay," whispered Dravid. "You have just taken medicine from Dr Vantargo. You were seriously ill."

The female started scratching the red sores on her face and arms and to the surprise of Dravid when she stopped the skin underneath had become perfectly soft and smooth.

The female felt her pockets, "Dalia, she's still sick, she must have this medicine," There was panic written all over her face. The woman ran to her house, followed by Higuain and Dravid.

Inside the house she leant over her sleeping daughter and stopped in mid action. "But how?" she turned and asked. "Her face, her skin: she is well again … but I haven't given her the medicine?" She stared at Higuain and Dravid, desperate for answers.

Higuain knelt by the child. "You have nothing to fear from us. My name is Higuain, my friend Dravid here, is a healer. He helped your daughter. We found her outside the town gate by the fountain, she was very ill."

"Thank you," she said grabbing his hand. "Thank you so much, you answered my prayers."

"What is your name?" asked Higuain, helping her to her feet.

"My name is Pesha, this is my daughter Dalia, and my husband, urm, he must still be outside."

"What happened here? Did Dr Vantargo do this to you all?"

"Oh no!" Pesha snapped. "He saved us. Without him the town would have been destroyed. About a month ago some of the people in the town started having sharp pains in their stomachs. Then their skin took on a green tint. It was at this point that the Doctor arrived in his carriage and told us of an evil virus that was sweeping through the continent. He said it was in the air, but he had a cure. He treated those who were sick for free. It was a miracle, they were saved.

"He told us that we would need to be treated every few days, but he would have to charge for the ingredients. As you can see by the state of the town, all the money is nearly gone. Pretty soon there will be nothing left and I, I don't know what will happen then. Please, I must find my husband. I will make some food to say thank you for what you have done for Dalia."

Dravid touched her wrist. "May I see the medicine?"

Pesha pulled it out of her pocket and looked at the green cloudy juice. "I bought this for my daughter. It's the last of my money. I will need it again if I start feeling ill."

He smiled. "It's okay, I will return it, I promise. I merely wish to see what it is."

She reluctantly handed over the vial and walked outside.

Dravid whispered, "I don't like this. I've never heard of such a virus. I've certainly not seen one act the way that just did. We need to keep an eye on this for a few more days. I don't trust Dr Vantargo. He may have painted himself as a saviour, but there is something not right about him."

Higuain looked at Dravid, "Where's Stratos?"

"I don't know. He was here before we went outside."

From the kitchen came a loud crash and the sound of pots and pans falling to the floor. They went to see what had happened. Stratos was on the floor groaning in pain and clutching his stomach.

"Stratos?" Dravid shook his head. "He has somehow caught the virus. His skin is green and he's in severe pain."

"Can't you give him the medicine from the doctor?" asked Higuain.

"No. I don't know what it is and I'm afraid we will need a more permanent solution and quickly. Because of his powers the virus is eating through his cells at a greater speed, three times faster than a normal human and I am nowhere near strong enough to heal him. For his size I will need all my strength, but Dalia drained me."

CHAPTER 14

Jimmy leapt out of bed at the sound of hammering on his bedroom door. Rubbing his eyes and staggering in the darkness, he collided with a small table and with a yelp hopped the rest of the way. Opening the door Jimmy was startled by the damaged face staring back at him. This was not a face he was expecting so early in the morning.

"My master," Majordomo wheezed, "I apologise for the early intrusion, but I've been requested to fetch you all. You are required in Professor Arual's class immediately for a field trip. Please pack your bag accordingly."

"Where are we going?" Jimmy asked.

Majordomo wheezed and then grinned, showing his yellow teeth. He strode off, his metal talon feet clanking on the floor.

Jimmy was the first into the classroom and sat at his seat looking out of the window over the drawbridge toward Elksidian Forest. Jimmy could feel a draft, so he wrapped his robe tighter around his shoulders. Jimmy glanced around the room and suddenly noticed what he assumed were picture frames were actually small mirrors. Jimmy approached the first picture immediately saw that his reflection was missing. Instead it was replaced by the image of a man in a tweed coat moving around a chalk board doing advanced mathematical sums. Jimmy turned behind him but there was no one there. The reflection of the man was captured within the mirror.

The second mirror he walked to was of a lone female sitting at a piano apparently singing her heart out. He remembered how his father used to try and sing opera flailing his arms around like this woman was.

Angry thoughts suddenly swelled uninvited into his head. He had buried the anger and rage deep but could feeling them bubbling to the surface.

Closing his eyes and breathing deeply a warm sensation tingled in his chest when he remembered his father sneaking into his bedroom late at night on what must have been his sixth birthday and giving him a colourful, beautifully wrapped present. Jimmy remembered the joy and excitement as a lone tear dripped down his cheek. He remembered another time when his mother had gone out for the day and, against her strict instructions, they had been out to the zoo where he won a small stuffed toy lion, just for trying. He reached inside his inner robe pocket and stroked the soft mane of the dirty old toy as another tear trickled from his eye.

A movement outside caught his attention. He stood to look out the window, and saw a strange bearded man standing at the entrance to the forest staring up at the castle. He wiped his eyes and studied the man, who turned and disappeared into the undergrowth. Jimmy waited for a few moments and was surprised to see Lyreco following the bearded man in great haste across the bridge and into the woodland.

"Jimmy Threeeepwood!" shouted a high-pitched voice followed by a series of hiccups. "I hope you have packed something warm. I have a fantastic field trip planned for you all, it will be so much fun, you will be meeting the ghoul contacts in the mortal world. They can sell you everything you will ever need," said Professor Arual.

"But Professor," Jimmy asked, "wasn't Professor Tinker supposed to be teaching us that?"

One by one the three other children arrived in the classroom.

"Never mind that, Jimmy, Professor Tinker has … urm … been unexpectedly … delayed. Now, I've spoken to Lord Trident and the Elders and once this field trip is concluded they seek your counsel. They wish to discuss with you your forthcoming journey to locate the Elixir of Light."

Jimmy's heart sank, he knew what was coming. They were all going to surely find out that he had given the scroll to help Higuain and Argon.

Professor Arual continued. "I've been to the library to collect the scroll but the Librarian …'

Oh no what I have done! I need to get ready; this must be a trap, I bet they already know, thought Jimmy anxiously.

"… has told me that one of you is very keen and has already collected the scroll and knows the exact location of where you need to start your quest. Well done, Jimmy."

Harry shook his head and whispered, "Swot."

"Right class (*hiccup*) if you are all ready we can get going. I need something first so let's go to the drawbridge. Come on, (*hiccup*) don't waste time."

Feeling in his pocket Jimmy touched the piece of paper he had scribbled a copy of the map on. *Madam Shrill. She covered for me. That was close. I'm going to have to use this copy and hope they don't ask to see the real version.*

Jimmy smiled at Talula. He wanted to talk to her but Professor Arual impatiently clapped her hands and shooed them all out through the door.

The group followed Professor Arual as she waddled through the castle grounds stopping midway on the wooden drawbridge. The thick black sea swirled below them.

Rummaging in her cloak pockets, the professor whipped out her thin, twig-like wand and a can of red Tomato soup. Turning to the group she put a finger to her bright pink lips, "Shhhh, I need silence. I know you have seen this trick before."

She took a deep breath and raised her arms high above her head, closed her eyes and rotated the wand in long circles.

Black angry clouds formed in the sky casting a veil of darkness over the castle grounds as the air became stale and cold. The professor continued painting the air with methodical up and down strokes. The black sea became unsettled as large waves splashed onto the grassy bank. Harry walked behind the Professor and gripped the wooden banister tightly. He bent over and peered into the water.

The floating white spirits were being suppressed by an invisible force as a whirlpool materialised and spun in the water, burrowing deeper and deeper into the sandy bed. With a flick of her wrist, Professor Arual made a small silver fish shoot out of the water flying high into the air. Gravity dragged it back down and its wet scales sparkled in all the colours of the rainbow when a beam of intense sunlight broke through the clouds.

Waving her wand and hands like a conductor in an orchestra Arual grasped the tin can and then threw it high into the air. The group watched but had to cover their eyes from the reflection as the can flew directly in line with the sun. The can fell next to the fish, the Professor dropped to her knees, thrust out her wand and shouted,

"Meeellllaaaatoooola!"

An intense red light filled the air, blocking out the sun while temporarily blinding the group. Harry held his hands over his eyes, the smell of singed magma drifted up his nostrils followed by a *plop* sound in the water next to him.

The children stared at Professor Arual who was pointing at the spot in the water where the whirlpool had been. The water bubbled and rumbled then slowly started to part, and a dripping, oil-covered pointed metal object rose out of the water.

In amazement the group stepped back with their mouths hanging open as a gigantic ship tore through the mud and pushed its way up the grassy bank. The magnificent red ship was covered in a thick, greasy substance that dripped back into the water, revealing more of the ship's metal body. The ship skidded to a stop and an enormous metal anchor fell from the side splashing into the water and crashing into the sea bed.

(*Hiccup*) "Well, my students, what do you think of the transport?"

With the snap of her fingers, a walkway skidded from the vessel bumping onto the wooden bridge.

"Come on," said Professor Arual, and waddled up the walkway onto the main deck of the boat.

Before the children had a chance to look around, the Professor made her way to the front of the boat and climbed a set of steps that took her high above the deck and onto an uncovered navigation bridge. She gripped a giant wooden wheel, which looked completely out of place on a modern boat of this type.

"Hold on tight!" she shouted and cranked a tall lever forward.

The ship roared and rumbled, and the engines burst to life. The rear propellers scraped and squealed, and the ship jerked forward but stopped. The Professor pulled back the lever then thrust it forward once more, grinding gears. Once more the ship jerked but nothing happened.

Percy leant over the side and shouted, "The anchor is still in the water."

Embarrassed, the Professor hiccupped, waved her wand and the anchor disengaged from its resting place. As soon as it was free the ship burst from the bank at great speed causing Jimmy to stagger backwards. He grabbed a post to steady himself. A thin yellow gel substance melted over the boat and Jimmy knew it was a perception filter that made them invisible to the mortals.

Jimmy watched the back of the boat and he could see the giant anchor being dragged behind, crashing into the floor and tearing up the road. He kept his head down and held on with all his strength.

CHAPTER 15

The giant ship ground to a halt on the outskirts of a large city centre and pulled into a layby, scraping past two parked cars leaving a long red scratch on their paint work and setting off their alarms. The group left the boat while the Professor made sure the coast was clear. With a double tap of her wand the boat collapsed in on itself shrinking and morphing back into the shape of a red tomato soup can. The lid flipped open and two beady fish eyes stared back up at her.

With a flick of her wand and puff of smoke, the fish sprouted wings, feet and a beak and transformed into a bird. Uncomfortably flapping its new wings, the bird soared into the sky.

The children and Professor Arual strolled through the centre of the bustling metropolis, passing shops of all shapes and sizes on either side of the road. One shop caught Talula's eye. It was filled with colourful tubs of sweets in every flavour imaginable. As she passed the open door, the shop keeper, dressed in a red and white uniform, smiled, showing his pearly white teeth.

Elbowing her way through the crowds of people Professor Arual glanced over her shoulder and spoke.

"This is the first stop," she said, pointing across the street at a dowdy old-fashioned clock maker with a dusty sign rocking in the breeze which read, 'It's Our Time.' The dilapidated old shop was completely out of place in between the futuristic shopfronts made of glass. Each store window displayed a plasma screen image listing sale products and general offers.

Panting heavily and hiccupping at every other word the Professor said, "This shop has been here for centuries and was the first on this road. These newer more fashionable shops have sprung up, but they will never outsell old Mr Gibbs and his rare and perfect time pieces. They are renowned all over the world. For us magic folk, he has been known to make **'special'** watches. But only if he likes you and believe me that is a very rare occurrence."

She pushed open the door and a quaint bell jingled. A giant of a man rose from his seat behind the counter. His gaunt face was thin and bony, he had sagging bags under his eyes and abnormally long arms that extended to the floor.

"Yessss?" he boomed.

Harry smiled elbowing Percy in the ribs and whispering "I bet he is one of the ghoul contacts we have come to meet."

"Arrhh Clairence," a professional-sounding voice came from the back room. From behind the counter, a young man with tiny round glasses hanging off the end of his nose, appeared. He sported a bright yellow polka-dot bow tie and a tool pouch dangled from his shirt pocket with a number of tiny metal tools sticking out.

"Mr Gibbs," said Professor Arual.

"Clairence Arual, how long has it been? Looking delightful as ever. And you've brought some new recruits. It can't be that time already, how time flies."

He lifted a section of the counter and walked into the main shop area. He studied the children with a grimace. "Bit scrawny aren't they, this new bunch? Not like the last lot, now they were special, hmm, except the owl one of course." He laughed but Jimmy detected a sinister undertone.

"Be nice, Mr Gibbs. If you remember, you didn't care for the last lot either."

Mr Gibbs clapped his hands at the giant man with long dragging arms.

"Terrence, I need urm, some supplies. Take this list and I'll see you in a few hours."

The giant man, Terrence, rolled his eyes and snatched the list then exited the shop to the sound of the jingling bell.

Once he was out of sight, Mr Gibbs walked to the windows and pulled down the blackout blind leaving only the slightest gap at the bottom to allow sunlight in. He grasped both sides of his head firmly and turned it sharply to the left, then to the right. A hiss of gas and a spray of air puffed out of the sides of his neck. He pulled his head loose from his neck and clutched it closely to his chest.

The group, frozen in place, regarded Mr Gibbs with wonder.

Now that he had removed his fake head, they could see his real one was no more than the size of a baseball. It was small, but had overly large sticky out ears. The real head was an exact copy of the fake head, except much smaller.

"What a relief!" said Mr Gibbs. "I'm glad you came in, it was getting warm in here and my new assistant Terrence sits there all day. I have to send him on errands just to get rid of him."

Harry was embarrassed and frustrated. He was sure Terence was the ghoul but by now he knew not to believe anything in this world.

"Mr Gibbs, we are only passing. I've brought the new students in for you to meet. These are Talula, Harry and Percy and last, but not least, Jimmy," she said pointing her wand in his direction.

Mr Gibbs looked them all up and down, licked his lips and spoke in a much squeakier voice.

"Jimmy Threepwood, aye. I've heard a lot about you."

Surprised, Jimmy cleared his throat and shrugged his shoulders.

"Now children, follow me. We have more people to meet and time is short," said Professor Arual, ushering them out of the shop.

As they each exited the shop Jimmy glanced back and saw Mr Gibbs' eyes following his every movement. As Jimmy went out into the street and walked past the neighbouring store he once again looked back and saw Mr Gibbs pull a shiny pocket watch out of his top pocket and hold it high in the air before pointing to Jimmy, then back at the watch.

That was odd, thought Jimmy. *Was he trying to say that watch was for me?*

Jimmy turned back and saw Talula was sweating, beads of perspiration growing on her forehead. Her skin looked almost green.

"I don't feel too great. I need to sit down," she muttered, but the Professor continued up ahead in the direction of the bustling town centre before arcing off toward a modern, bright blue phone shop. Jimmy saw the Professor open the door to let Harry and Percy into the store. Jimmy was about to try and catch up when he saw Talula stagger, lose her balance and fall, propping herself up against a wall.

*　　　*　　　*

Talula could feel herself getting warmer and warmer as beads of sweat dropped from her brow to the floor. *"Kill them, kill them all!"* rang in her ears.

She could feel her mind being pulled away from her and the image of a distant figure beckoning her to come to him. Struggling to control her mind, sweet, warming music soothed her followed by a calming voice, the same voice telling her to kill them.

"Let yourself go Talula, let your mind go." She shook her head, fighting against the voice and her body started to tremble. In fright she saw that her fingernails were no longer her own. They had grown long, and yellow and dried blood remained where they had pierced through the tips of her fingers.

Her body was going into shock and she grabbed the wall, but the more she fought against the voice the louder the music rang in her mind and the softer and more soothing it became.

"Let your mind go! Kill them, kill them all. They are not your friends. I can help you."

*　　　*　　　*

Jimmy knew something bad was happening to Talula. He touched her shoulder. In a flash, Talula swung her clawed hand fiercely at his face as her razor-sharp nails skimmed his cheek.

Jimmy stepped back as he felt the sharp stinging sensation on his face. Astonished, he stared at Talula and saw that her eyes had shrunken to beady pin holes above her nose and that two fangs were protruding from her top lip. He touched his burning right cheek and when he took his hand away, saw smeared blood on his fingers.

Talula clenched both of her shaking hands to the sides of her head and released a high pitched shrill.

"Arrrghh I can't fight him anymore; the music is too soothing, I can't …'

Hair started sprouting out of the back of her hands and her nose grew into a pig snout. Her boots burst open as monstrous clawed toes punctured the leather.

Without warning a spark flicked in her right claw and ignited into a pulsating ball of fire. She threw the fire ball, which rushed through the air, erupting on the glass window of the phone shop, which exploded sending glass shrapnel through the air.

"Talula!" shouted Jimmy "What's wrong?"

Talula's eyes flicked.

"Arrrgh, what are those creatures, they are everywhere!"

Jimmy spun around, scanning the area, but there was no one there. *What does she mean, 'creatures?' There's no else here!*

Talula roared and sent out wave after wave of green fireballs, which rained down causing the hundreds of people out shopping to run for their lives. Windows smashed, wooden stalls exploded, and roads were set alight in a blaze of destruction.

Professor Arual staggered out of the phone shop covered in glass and dust. Yanking her wand out of her cloak she fired an electric whip of light, which streamed over the beast's shoulder and sliced a delivery van in two.

The air was filled with the smell of fire and the sounds of fear and people screaming in panic. Professor Arual composed herself and pulled her wand back again for another assault. She flicked her wrist and as the beam projected out of her wand Jimmy dived through the air and knocked it away.

"You can't harm her. She's not in control of her mind. Something has a hold of her."

Talula staggered towards Jimmy and the Professor as snot and saliva dripped out of her snout and down her snarling fangs. With a high-pitched yelp, she raised her claws high above her head. Jimmy stared into her eyes and was sure he caught a glimpse of her human form trapped behind the glassy pupils desperate to escape.

Desperation flooded over him. "Talula, it's me, Jimmy."

The mighty claws thrashed through the air and he flinched. Talula pulled back at the last second, clearly fighting a powerful urge, and her arms trembled as she kept them locked at waist height.

"Arrgghh!" she screamed, shaking her head.

With one giant leap Talula sprang from the ground and landed high on top of the damaged buildings. Jimmy watched her scurrying back in the direction of Sepura Castle.

CHAPTER 16

C rickets chirped outside of the house and moonlight peered in though the uncovered windows.

"What do you think it is, Dravid?" asked Higuain, looking solemnly at her fallen companion. Stratos was resting on a mattress and groaning in pain. The stench in the house had become unbearable as the health of Pesha and her husband gradually deteriorated.

Dravid opened the vial for what seemed the hundredth time. The cork gave a small *pop* as it came loose.

"I just don't know. It has an odd powdery tinge. It smells like a pain suppressor. I can't distinguish anything else in there but colouring agent."

"What else can it be? It can't be the gas as we were exposed to that too and we're fine. What has Stratos had that we haven't? Why don't we give him the medicine to see what happens?"

"No!" Dravid snapped. "I don't trust that doctor. There could be anything in this. We must wait until my strength returns and then I'll heal him."

Higuain abruptly stood up accidently knocking the chair over, "He could be dead by then and so could Argon. I'm going to get some water, see if you can make him more comfortable."

Walking along the silent dusty road she felt a surge of sorrow and dread. All the houses she passed were dark and quiet. There had obviously been no upkeep in this village for months, what with all their money being given to Dr Vantargo for his medicine. Higuain felt guilt rumbling in her stomach at what she had just asked Dravid to do, but all she could think about was Argon and saving him.

On approaching the grand metal fountain, she was startled to see streams of water jetting out of the statue's body. She lifted her head, hearing rumbling wheels approaching in the distance. She crouched down and ran to the nearby forest that ran along the perimeter of the town. She ducked under a bush and peered through the leaves.

In the distance she could just about make out the outline of a carriage, but nothing more. Then, a robed figure scurried along the town wall towards the wooden framed entrance and like a ghost peered into the town. With the coast clear, the ghostly figure crept to the flowing fountain and after fumbling in his cloak's pockets, pulled out a glass vial filled with an illuminated pink fluid, and poured it into the churning water.

Higuain shifted her weight to get a better view and a twig snapped. The robed figure spun round and stared directly at where Higuain was hiding. She held her breath. *Can he see me? Why hasn't he run?* thought Higuain.

The figure rummaged again through his cloak, this time pulling out a sky-blue liquid. Flicking the glass with his finger he pulled off the lid and poured it into the fountain. The figure waited a few moments before pulling off his hood and smiling before scurrying off towards his carriage.

Fury boiled in Higuain. "Dr Vantargo! You've been poisoning the water then selling them the cure! You treacherous little snake." The anger surged around her body and each heart beat felt like it would explode out of her chest. Her eyes flickered bright crimson, illuminating the bush.

"You dare deceive these poor people and take their worldly goods!" she demanded.

Dr Vantargo turned and saw the red eyes pulsating in the woods. He took off as fast as his little legs would carry him. A circle of fire ignited around him, stopping him in his tracks. Higuain stepped out from behind her cover and confronted him.

Dr Vantargo fell to his knees and begged for forgiveness, his nose scrunched up like an animal.

"I'm sorry, I needed the money. It's harmless. The fluid makes them ill for two days and I spray the air with this orange powder and it makes them crave the medicine. I can reverse what I've done, I promise, please, please don't hurt me'

"You fool!" Higuain rasped. "You've caused great suffering to these people and you've made my companion ill. His magic cells are attacking his normal ones."

"I've a cure, not the one I've been selling to the people, that only lasts a few days, but a cure to fix them all. It's in my carriage."

Higuain waved her hand and the fire was extinguished. She stepped forward, grabbed the cowering man and propelled him towards the vehicle. With his nose twitching Dr Vantargo opened a hidden side compartment on his carriage, revealing twenty colourful glass vials.

"Which one?"

His lower lip quivered. "All, all, they all do the same thing."

Higuain scooped up the bottles and dragged them into Vantargo's empty rucksack. They clanked together in the bottom of the bag. Reaching in deeper to grab the last vial her hand touched six hard large leather sacks.

"What do we have here, then?" She pulled out the heavy bags and saw that each was filled to the brim with glistening gold coins.

"No, no please, that's my life savings."

"I feel the townsfolk are due some compensation for the trouble you've caused them." Higuain thrust the heavy bags into Dr Vantargo's stomach, knocking his breath away. "You carry this money and give it back to them once I've administered the cure. Then I will decide what to do with you."

Higuain sat beside the doctor while he drove the colourful carriage into the middle of the town. Dr Vantargo pressed a large green button and with a loud bang, plumes of orange smoke wafted into the air and flowed through windows and gaps under doors. Within seconds the zombielike townsfolk, including Pesha, her husband and even the mighty Stratos, staggered outside. Dravid appeared in the doorway and when he saw Higuain firmly holding Dr Vantargo he joined her to find out what had happened.

"I caught him," she said. "I caught him putting a fluid in the water to make them ill!"

"I knew there was something not right about this," Dravid said, sneering at the grovelling doctor as he dropped to the floor and cowered against the carriage wheels.

"Here, give them this. It's the cure," said Higuain, passing him the vials.

Within seconds of drinking the fluid the colour returned to the faces of the townsfolk and their temperatures returned to normal. Although they were weak and exhausted they called to Higuain demanding an explanation.

"People of Pickington, the virus that was infecting you has been cured. It seems your saviour, Dr Vantargo, was poisoning you. He was placing a substance in the water to make you ill, so you would buy his medicine."

The townsfolk roared in anger, raising fists in the air.

"Dr Vantargo has kindly agreed to return all of your money and will include a little bonus for the trouble."

Dr Vantargo stared up from the dusty floor with an expression which clearly read, 'will I?'

With a gentle kick from Higuain he jumped to his feet, grabbed the bags of gold and moved reluctantly to the first person. The first resident snarled and hit him around the head, grabbed a handful of gold and walked off.

Once all the money was returned the first rays of the morning sun filled the air.

Stratos was waiting for his chance. Grabbing the scrawny doctor by his collar he lifted him high into the air.

"What shall we do with him?" Stratos roared. "Put him in the stocks? Throw him in prison?"

The town chanted and screamed in appreciation.

"No, no, Stratos," said the calming voice of Dravid. "I have a greater punishment to fit his crime."

Stratos dropped the snivelling doctor to the floor. Dravid smiled, whispering unusual words that danced on the morning breeze. Dr Vantargo began wiggling his nose uncontrollably. His eyes were darting from left to right, whiskers sprouted from his cheeks and a fluffy tail tore through his trousers. With a puff of smoke, he shrank down into a weasel that fitted comfortably into Dravid's hand.

The disorientated weasel scampered around Dravid's hand sniffing and wiggling its nose.

"If you want to act like a weasel, you can be one," said Dravid, tucking him into his cloak pocket.

CHAPTER 17

Talula, in the form of the beast, chewed up the ground and charged through Elksidian Forest in the direction of Sepura Castle. Reaching the wooden bridge, she clattered over the wooden beams just as her companions and Dr Arual, led by Jimmy, emerged from the forest.

*   *   *

"What's wrong with her?" shouted Percy, panting heavily.

"I don't know," said Jimmy frantically. "She just started to morph into a bat, but something was holding her back. I think something, or someone is controlling her actions and changing her into that creature. Come on! She's in the castle grounds."

They burst through the entrance sliding on the hard stone floors as the stale smell engulfed them once more. Jimmy could feel the cold and dampness of the castle seeping into his bones and it sent a chill racing down his spine. There was no sign of Talula, but Jimmy saw Majordomo slumped in the corner buried under a mountain of old castle armour with a giant shield pinning him to the floor.

Percy and Jimmy rushed over and dragged the heavy metal off him. The butler wheezed, struggling for breath.

"I was attacked from behind," he rasped. "I was stuck by a claw. Whatever it was it went to the gardens." His eyes closed, and he gasped for air.

"Professor!" Jimmy shouted. "You look after him; we'll go after Talula."

Before Professor Arual had time to respond the three boys ran to the staircase and with a wobbling, slurping sound were sucked into the castle's void.

Re-appearing out of the ground the group landed in a swampy, foul smelling sludge, which covered their legs up to their knees. They were deep in the castle's garden, somewhere they'd not been before. Gagging at the smell, the three boys waded through the thick mud, every step sinking in further and further. Harry moaned, dragging his foot forward. As he did so his boot became lodged and he lost his footing before falling face first into the mire. In panic, he splashed his arms and managed to stand upright. He dragged the muck off his face and flicked it onto the floor.

"Purrgh, what is this stuff?" shouted Harry. "It stinks like rotten eggs." He groaned, pulling a face, trying desperately to clear his nostrils and tugging at the thick grey sludge drying in his hair. "Get me out of here," he yelled, holding out his sludge-covered arms for help.

Percy and Jimmy finally reached the end of the swamp.

Jimmy darted off into the shrubbery and pulled out a long wooden stick. He stretched it out over the sludge close enough for Harry to reach. Harry gripped the stick and the two boys managed to finally drag him out. Harry clambered up the bank and wiped his filthy socks on the forest floor. Scrunching his nose up he pulled his boot back on and the three of them gazed at the wildly overgrown castle gardens ahead.

The warm air was abuzz with insects and pollen. The boys could sense that the overgrown, jungle-like garden, was alive with eyes staring back at them and scurrying insects all around them, in the bushes and trees.

"Wow, look at this place!" said Percy, in awe at the wild explosion of colours and giant plant leaves blocking their path.

"There!" shouted Jimmy, pointing to a trail of trampled bushes and recently shredded shrubs. "That must be where she's gone. Come on!"

As Jimmy spoke the final word, a green vine whipped through the trees and before he had time to react entangled his feet and whisked him high into the air. Six more vines with sharp protruding thorns wrapped tightly around his wrists, mouth and body, snaking around him and cocooning him suspended in mid-air.

Percy and Harry stared up at Jimmy, but vines slithered towards their feet from either side of the undergrowth as well. Percy responded by instinctively releasing a wave of continuous fire that ignited the vine nearest him, sending a trail of fire throughout the garden as the singed vine thrashed in pain. Harry created an intense fireball and sent it spiralling through the air. The vine that was attacking him disintegrated leaving behind a small plume of smoke.

They both flinched as a high-pitched shriek sounded behind them, from somewhere beyond deep within the swamp.

A gigantic tree towering above them started flailing its branches around and a grumbling noise came from a large slit in the bottom of the bark, which began to move, like a mouth. The tree stopped moaning and a thousand green vines, each one with the head of a snake, hissed. The first snake-vine pounced forward with its fangs exposed. Percy dived out of the way and released a stream of red hot fire which instantly consumed it.

Harry's palm sparked ready to create a fireball, but a vine appeared over his shoulder and ensnared his wrist. Three more entangled his legs and body. Despite struggling with all his might, the plant's grip tightened until it had dragged him to the floor and cocooned him.

Percy saw his companion fall and the distraction was all the tree needed. A snake-headed vine whipped below the flames and latched on to his neck piercing his skin with its plant venom. As the teeth punctured Percy's skin, the warm fluid flooded his body. His vision wavered and he lost his balance. He collapsed, and the vines ensnared his body.

*   *   *

Jimmy was suspended high in the air upside down feeling the vines squeezing tighter and crushing his body. His mouth was completely covered, and he struggled for breath. His vision clouded, and he saw his friends fall one by one below him.

Jimmy was trapped but knew he had to rescue Talula. He had to finish his training and avenge his father's death. His blood felt as though it was boiling within him, and the more he thought about his father the angrier he became. Beads of sweat started dripping down his forehead. The burning sensation was unbearable, and he felt the vines crushing his chest and throat. In an instant, an intake of fresh air flooded into his lungs and he smelled fire.

Opening his eyes, he saw with a jolt that his whole body was alight with intense green flames that illuminated the overshadowed garden. The vines around him were ablaze with fire and he was free, hovering high in the air transformed into a flaming phoenix.

The anger swelled in his stomach and he felt his inner monster wrestling and trying to force its way out. His companions were in trouble too and Talula was getting away.

Jimmy swooped downward, flying with all his strength and slicing through the plants leaving a trail of fire in his wake. Thrusting his wings out, the momentum propelled him through the mouth of the tree. He tore through the middle of it and burst out of the top.

The trail of green fire burnt through the core of the tree, it imploded sending high pitched screams echoing throughout the garden.

Jimmy swooped down, freed his companions from the lifeless plants and helped them to their feet.

"Are you both okay?" he asked, his skin still glowing green and his clothes smelling of singed fabric.

Percy grabbed his puncture wound and grumbled "Yeah … just. That was impressive."

Harry dusted off the dead vines and they fell to the floor. "Yeah. That thing was crushing my chest. I couldn't move."

"Come on, Talula went that way. We can rest later."

CHAPTER 18

Trampling through overgrown, waist high weeds along a slushy, muddy trail, Jimmy followed Talula's large footprints, as they made their way through the garden.

Suddenly, without warning the forest ended and they emerged in a large circular opening covered with luscious green grass. In the centre of the opening was the tall, rickety wooden bell tower that Jimmy could see from his bedroom window. The spire of the tower shot up into the clouds and gently swayed from side to side in the breeze. Jimmy noticed that the wooden frame was decayed and that the rotten panels had fallen away so that they could see straight through sections of the tower, all the way to the top. The boys spotted Talula halfway up the stairs. Jimmy could see Talula squeezing her head as though in pain through the large hole in the top of the tower before she roared and disappearing out of view.

The three boys ran to the entrance.

Jimmy pulled open the wooden door and a gust of wind brushed their faces.

"Whoa!" shouted Percy. "This tower isn't stable! Did you feel the way it rocked and moved? That was only a little puff of wind."

Another strong gust of wind blew past and as they looked upwards, the whole tower shuffled to one side with a mighty creak and small shards of wood fell from high above them.

"That's a long way to fall," said Harry. "Especially if the whole thing collapses and I don't think it's got too much time left in it."

"Talula is up there. We must help her. She would do the same for you. Let's go!" shouted Jimmy.

Jimmy stepped on the first wooden step and it cracked under his weight.

"Completely rotten," said Percy picking up the wood and inspecting it. It crumbled in his hand. "This is a bad idea."

Determined, Jimmy kicked the second piece of wood making sure it was solid and with caution climbed the steps. He could see the giant, bronze bell suspended directly above them.

Carefully navigating each step, the three boys made it to the top and peered out of the small window that ran alongside the steps.

"This is really high, I can see for miles, said Harry, approaching the edge with trepidation.

At the top of the steps, they entered a damp, dusky square room and saw the giant bell hanging from a thick wooden beam.

Talula was standing mid-way along the room, hissing and snarling. A man draped in long black robes with the cowl covering his face was standing directly behind her.

"What have you done to her?" demanded Jimmy. Harry's hands ignited ready for action.

The hooded man pulled back his cowl to reveal a man in his late forties with a shrivelled, pig-like face with two thick yellow fangs sticking out of his top lip.

"You!" shouted Jimmy, "… from the book."

Harry and Percy looked at him in surprise.

"You know him?" asked Percy.

The man grunted and laughed sounding like a pig snort.

"Jimmy Threepwood and his band of misfits. I've waited a long time for this day."

"Who are you?" Jimmy shouted.

"Of course," replied the pig-man. "You may not have heard of me. I've been simply forgotten." He clenched his fist. "I wasn't a great hero that tried to wreck the plan. I was the fool who helped them. And for what?" he shouted. "To be lied to and cast away like dirt. Since the day I was forced into hiding, I've struck fear into the world living as Crinder, or as you know me, Jimmy … the Chiroptera Charmer. I was once the companion of Aurabella, Argon and …"

"You were one of the last children?" asked Percy, stopping Crinder in mid flow.

"Yes, one of the chosen four. What an honour that was. Before I had to hide and live in the shadows I had a real name. I was a real boy, Vesty VanMartin. But I've had a long time to exact my revenge on the Elders for what they did to me."

"Stop! Why Talula, what have you done to her?" pleaded Jimmy.

A maniacal smile spread across Crinder's face. "Foolish child. Do you not know what a Chiroptera Charmer is? I have total control of any bat. They have no choice but to do my bidding and you have all seen Talula's inner creature, so I can control her very soul. I've spent years and years learning this skill and now she is mine."

No, he can't do this: I need to buy some time to find out more about how he is controlling her and what his plan is, thought Jimmy.

"But what can Talula do to help you?"

"I will use her powers along with my own to force open the gate and release Tyranacus. Together we will destroy the council and rule this world as I was once promised."

"But how can you open the gate? It will take all four of us, not just one," retorted Harry.

The hooded man reached down the back of his robe and pulled out the golden flute. "I know a way," he snarled, and he pressed the flute to his mouth. He blew, releasing a flurry of tantalising music that bounced off the wooden walls.

Talula snarled like a rabid dog. She groaned and stamped forward swinging her clawed hands. Percy stood ready to attack.

"No!" shouted Jimmy. "You can't attack her. Vesty's controlling her."

Harry ignited his hands and dived to the side of Talula so that he could get a clear view of the hooded man. A stream of fiery rage discharged from his clenched fists. Vesty lowered the flute and deflected the fire with his right forearm. It ricocheted, setting the closest panel and ceiling alight.

"Fool! This tower is made of wood, you will kill us all."

A sinister expression overshadowed Harry's face as his true soul boiled to the surface. "So be it!" he shouted. "You'll meet the same demise as us."

Vesty was trying to use Talula to block their path. Her toenails scratched the wood floor and she lurched towards Jimmy. Her claws slashed Jimmy's chest, slicing through his skin. Jimmy stepped backward just in time to avoid the second swipe.

"Talula, stop! You need to fight this. He's controlling you. Fight it!"

Roaring, Talula staggered backward and Jimmy saw that the beast was starting to lose control in the power struggle with its inner soul. But Talula was still under the influence and muttered, "He's in danger. Must kill the boy with fire. Kill him, kill him ...."

She swung her attention away from Jimmy and sprang through the air towards Harry, catching him off guard. The impact sent him crashing through the wooden banister. His head struck the wall knocking him unconscious. Talula's claws pinned him to the ground, she raised her right claw above her head for the final strike and time stood still as she slashed downward.

Jimmy was frozen to the spot. He couldn't hurt Talula and that's what it would have taken to stop her.

"Talula, nooooo!"

The silence erupted in a blaze of fire as Talula's chest exploded and the girl was thrown backwards. Singed flesh and fur wafted around the room. Talula lay silently on her back with smoke drifting from her chest. Percy watched, his hands still smouldering from the fireball. He faced Jimmy.

"I'm sorry, Jimmy, I had to, she would have killed Harry. I had no choice," said Percy.

Jimmy saw the cloaked atrocity backing into the corner of the blazing room, his eyes assessing the situation. He was trying to find an escape route.

The flames had taken hold of the wooden panels and plumes of thick black smoke filled the room. They coughed and covered their noses, trying to stop the black smoke from clogging their lungs. But Percy was focused on Vesty. With his hands sparking, waiting for them to ignite, he moved forward, his face twisted with evil.

The silent hand of the black smoke squeezed Jimmy's chest as he began to cough violently. His eyes stung, filled with water. Through the smoke Jimmy saw Percy approaching Vesty, his hands igniting into balls of flame.

Jimmy's head felt a gentle shower of ash dropping down. He looked up and saw that the beam supporting the ceiling was glowing red. Percy raised his hand to administer his revenge, the beam snapped, and the pillar crashed down, crushing Percy before smashing through the wooden floor obliterating sections of the stair case directly below.

"Percy!" Jimmy screamed. He tried to move, but it all happened too quickly.

Blood dripped from Percy's soot-covered face and he gasped for air. A large chunk of the floor, barely two inches next to his shoulder, was missing. The far wall burst into flames and in the same instant a gust of wind rocked the structure from side to side.

Jimmy staggered, placing his hand on the burning wood as the towering inferno swayed around him. He winced and pulled his burnt hand away, dropping to his knees. He could feel his heart racing and desperation flooded his mind. *There's no way out, Percy, Talula and Harry are injured. It's just me left*. In the corner of the room he saw Vesty smirking and lifting the flute to his mouth.

Pressing it to his lips the melody drifted through the smoke, reaching every corner of the tower. Talula's eyes flickered then opened, and she staggered to her feet. *She must be reacting to the music*, thought Jimmy. He wasn't even sure if she was awake, her movement was more like a puppet dancing on a string.

The music stopped and was replaced by a deathly laugh.

"This is the end for all of you, Jimmy Threepwood. Talula and I will release the beast and destroy the world together."

Coughing and wheezing, Jimmy saw Harry unconscious on the floor, and a dazed Percy trying to find his bearings. Jimmy watched Talula marching towards him and suddenly remembered the words of Majordomo.

That bell would ring twice a day signalling sunrise and sunset, but suddenly exactly one hundred years ago it just stopped. I've been up there a few times, but I cannot see what has happened.

"Vesty …." Jimmy stared at Vesty's pig-like face, then at Talula. They had the same features. Vesty's inner creature must have been some form of bat and he became stuck whilst morphing, just like Talula. That's why the bell stopped one hundred years ago. That's when he came here and started hiding …

A bolt of bright yellow lightning formed in Jimmy's hand. He threw it and it tore through the smoke exploding at the base of the giant bronze bell.

The bell rocked back and forth sending loud decibels through the castle grounds. Vesty and Talula grabbed their ears and screamed. Vesty staggered around the burning building, dragged off his robe and two bat wings unfurled. He screamed in pain and dived forward feet first, glided through the air and grabbed Talula by the shoulders. His nails dug into her flesh and he flapped his wings and crashed through the blazing panel. Jimmy ran to the hole in the wall and watched in terror. After initially diving into free fall over the edge Vesty compensated for the extra weight and flew off into the sunlight with Talula dangling below him.

The impact of Vesty smashing through the side caused the tower to topple, and as it collapsed Jimmy grabbed Harry, dragging him across the damaged floor, and propped him up in front of the hole. He dashed towards Percy, but the wood holding the bell was ablaze and collapsed. The bell hurtled downwards and disappeared through the floor below.

Percy was conscious but injured. Jimmy helped him up and they hobbled to Harry. The base of the tower gave way and the tower was sent spiralling to the floor. Using the momentum Jimmy grabbed Harry whilst still holding Percy and dived from the towering inferno. They plummeted down but before they could hit the ground, Jimmy morphed into the phoenix and gripped his two companions with his talons.

The force of the collapsing tower sent a stream of air across the struggling bird. Jimmy knew they were losing altitude and that he wouldn't be able to continue flying with the full weight of the two boys but all he could do was try to aim for the softest landing.

CHAPTER 19

With the ground fast approaching, the phoenix and the two boys collided with the top of a tree before crashing downwards, hitting branches as they fell. Although it was painful, the branches slowed their descent and the impact with the ground was minimal.

Breathing a deep sigh of relief, Jimmy saw the wreckage of the tower smouldering not far off. It finally collapsed to the ground, sending a tsunami of black soot and ash over the area. Jimmy coughed, his lungs clogged with thick black smoke. There was no time to waste. He could see Vesty flying off into the distance carrying Talula. He wanted to follow but his drained body surrendered, and he collapsed, his head buried in a mound of crisp leaves. "Don't worry, Talula, I'm coming for you …." he whispered.

"Wake up Jimmy, wake up! Percy's hurt," a distant voice sounded in Jimmy's ears. The voice grew louder and was then replaced by a continuous ringing then banging. He opened his eyes and the sunlight bored into his skull. He grabbed the front of his head and checked for blood. It felt as though he had been hit with a hammer. Opening his eyes again Harry came into focus. He was standing nearby, covered from head to toe in black dust. His robes and clothing had been torn to shreds and dozens of small bloody cuts and gashes were visible all over his body.

"Snap out of it, Jimmy, come on: Percy's hurt!" shouted Harry taking hold of his shoulder and helping him to his feet.

Although his head was pounding, Jimmy staggered behind Harry and dropped to his knees in front of the injured Percy

"Look at his leg, there's a thick stake of wood buried in there and it's in deep. I'm not pulling that out. What are we going to do? He can't walk."

Percy was awake, his face was white, and his body trembled as he started going into shock. Reaching forward, Jimmy wrapped his fingers around the thick piece of wood.

"We don't know how long this is. We need to get him back. We'll have to carry him."

"That's not all," said Harry, "Can you smell that? Look at the skin, it's turning grey. I think the flesh is dying." He poked Percy's leg with his finger and a small dry section fell off onto the floor and yellow pus oozed out.

"Grab his arm, Harry; we have to get him back quick. I don't like the look of this."

Dragging Percy through the gardens was exhausting. They staggered towards the rear entrance of the castle and Harry reached out to the door handle, but the door suddenly opened and Majordomo towered above them. His breath made a nasty wheezing sound caused by small pockets of air leaking out of the damaged skin under his cheeks.

"Massster Percy," he gasped, and reached out his thin white-gloved hands to assist the boys. "We need to get him to the nurse. Please, masters." Jimmy noticed a white bandage wrapped around his head from where Talula had hit him as she entered the castle. "I will take Master Percy to the nurse. You musssst rest and clean up. I will collect you as soon as I have any news."

Before either of the boys had time to reflect, the ravaged butler whisked Percy off.

Harry touched the multitude of small cuts and abrasions on his chest and said, "Come on, Jimmy, we can't do any more for him. Let the nurse fix him up and we'll speak to Lyreco to find out how Talula and Vesty can free Tyranacus without all of us being there."

Nodding, Jimmy hobbled towards the closest staircase. Pain and exhaustion were catching up with him. Every movement felt like a thousand tiny needles poking into his head and he could barely feel the rest of his body. He staggered up the stairs and headed for his room, but his mind was focused on one thing … finding Talula, and quickly.

* * *

Icy air ran down Xanadu's back and passed through the thin strands of greasy, long, black hair. She snarled and showed her tiny, sharp yellow teeth. Up ahead, the flaming torch held by Majordomo flickered as his clanking clawed feet climbed the stone steps leading to the highest point of the castle, the keep, or as it had been named centuries before, the Vantage Room. The cavernous space still had remnants of its former glory during a bygone age when it housed the Elders in their human forms. Patches of gold and emeralds could be seen along the walls and the air was tainted with a faint hint of magma or brimstone coming from deep within a sealed gorge hidden next to the stairs.

Xanadu leaned towards the edge of the steps next to the sheer drop, and disturbed small piles of dust and rubble. It spiralled over the lip, crashing into the cavern structure before falling into silence. She peered over the edge but all she could see was a void. Snarling, Xanadu pushed herself away from the edge and scurried after her guide, keeping close to the damp wall.

Reaching the last step of the spiralling staircase Xanadu watched as Majordomo staggered, propping his weary body against the wall and gasping for air. Whilst breathing, it looked as though each breath was through a straw and someone was squeezing the end. "I must hurry, Xanadu," coughed Majordomo, "I have to attend to Percy." Snarling, she snatched the flickering torch from his hand and approached the two stone doors, one to her left and one directly ahead. She pulled a crumpled brown map from her pocket and held it close to the naked flame, marrying her location with the layout of the castle.

"Majordomo," she snapped. "You fool! These are simply stone doors, there is nothing behind them. Look!" She thrust the map into his face. "Beyond the doors is nothing but fresh air," she kicked the wall to her left and threw the map onto the floor.

Majordomo didn't flinch. He was lost in a trance, staring longingly over the edge of the staircase into the blackness. He gazed through a mist in his mind, down at his metal clawed feet and inhaled deeply into his scarred, damaged lungs. An expression of sadness flickered across his scarred face. Glancing upward he noticed the three-inch-tall, gold remains of what was once the metal guard rail.

Majordomo lowered the flame illuminating the wall and Xanadu saw a perfect carving of a large rose spreading from top to bottom. She ran her fingers over the creation, which though perfectly smooth, harboured a dark, sinister presence behind it.

"No, Xanadu," wheezed the butler as he eased himself upright and moved forward. "To see the Elders, you must first look." He limped forward, and he pulled her away from the door on the left. "That is the Rose Door. Beyond this lies the ultimate, most sacred power in the universe. Even I have never seen what lies in there."

Escorting her to the door in front of them he whispered, "Close your eyes and think of Lord Trident," and pulled her over the threshold.

CHAPTER 20

Jimmy dropped through the ceiling and landed softly on the ground below. Standing in the hallway near to his bedroom door, images of Talula and Vesty rushed through his mind. The most vivid memory was the foul monster flying through the cauldron of fire and grabbing Talula before pulling her away from the tower. *She was right in front of me, right there, why didn't I grab her?* A second voice, a voice of reason spoke. *She is a wild animal, she was trying to kill you. If you had grabbed her Vesty would have escaped and you could never have saved all your friends.*

"Arrgh!" screamed Jimmy, and punched the wall beside him. The chunk of wall exploded under his hand sending a pile of rubble to the carpeted floor.

Realising what he had done, Jimmy stepped away from the wall and ran his hands over his face then through his hair. He stared at his decaying hands. They had become worse since he returned to the castle. His skin had an even darker tinge to it and was now dry and flaky with his veins more noticeable. Turning away, Jimmy was just about to sink into the floor to find Lyreco, when he noticed wet footprints, still fresh, leading under his bedroom door. He scrutinised the prints and realised they were human, maybe belonging to a child. With trepidation he crept to the door, over the creaking wooden floor boards and slowly opened it, shedding light into the darkened room. To his surprise he saw the mirror image of himself sitting on the edge of his bed.

Jimmy stepped back in amazement and his hands automatically sparked into life and a fierce light came into his now pure obsidian eyes.

"Wait, Jimmy, please!" the second Jimmy shouted. 'I'm not here to harm you, I promise! Please, think back to the day you arrived at Sepura Castle. The shadowy creature pulled you into the water, you couldn't breathe, you were drowning."

Thoughts swam around Jimmy's mind as he remembered a vision of himself outlined in the water. The vision had pulled the black soul off him and helped him to the surface.

The crackling in his hands faded. Jimmy stepped forward and through a sliver of light shining in through the curtains, the figure in front of him was revealed. It was a young boy in the image of Jimmy with the same robes and phoenix badge, everything the same, down to the mop of ginger hair. One thing was clearly different; he was made of clear, translucent liquid, which was visible flowing through his body.

"Who, what are you?" Jimmy demanded.

The mirror image rose from the bed and spoke in a soft, comforting voice, "Jimmy, I am you! Well, a part of you at least. Think back to the day shortly after your father died and you returned to Elksidian Forest. You were learning a conjuring spell, but you were not ready. You were too overwhelmed with sadness and anger and you kept repeating the spell over and over."

Jimmy stared into his mirror image's eyes, then rubbed his left hand. "I felt something being ripped from my body, a transparent phantom … you!"

The image spoke softly, "That was the day your world came crashing down around you. You were so filled with rage, sadness and revenge that you forced your goodness out of your body leaving only this twisted, power mad version of yourself.

I am that goodness, Jimmy, and I will never leave you. I just hope that one day your path will become clearer and you and I can merge back together.

"But you need to look at yourself, Jimmy. This obsession with revenge will cause the destruction of this beautiful world because your judgement is too clouded with hate."

Anger engulfed Jimmy's eyes and his whole body caught alight with the intensely burning green flame.

The anger resonated in his voice. "Then so be it! You are not part of me! How can you be? That monster took away the only person that ever cared for me and for what? Just because he could. Well, no more! I will not rest until the Gatekeeper has been destroyed and I will gather every piece of power I can until that has been achieved."

"But …'

"There is no but. I will see this through to the end and if you try to stop me, I will destroy you as well."

"I will leave you now, Jimmy, but I will be watching you. Be careful, I've a feeling that not everything is as it seems." Smiling once more the image melted into a silver fluid puddle and drained away through the cracks of the floor.

Jimmy threw himself down onto his bed and as he relaxed the fire was calmed. The words were flashing through his mind, *I know I am right. He must be punished for what he has done, regardless of the cost.*

CHAPTER 21

Warm, clean, air flooded Xanadu's nasal passage. She opened her eyes and the brightly lit Vantage Room slowly came into focus.

With her eyes adjusting, she looked down and her heart leapt into her mouth. There was no floor. She was walking on clear blue sky high above the ground. Fluffy white clouds drifted through the air and past her feet. Xanadu crouched down to touch the clouds with her clawed fingers, and it was soft, a gentle stream of warm air swirling around her fingers. Directly below she saw that she was suspended at the highest point of the Castle, which she knew was invisible to the naked eye from the ground. *That's why the map didn't show a room behind the door. It doesn't exist.*

She spun round to face Majordomo and showed her teeth, "Why didn't you tell me about the floor?" she snarled.

He breathed heavily and avoided eye contact, but a small smile crossed his face.

"Mistress Xanadu; you were in such a hurry. I didn't feel we had time to discuss the situation thoroughly."

Scowling, Xanadu stepped through a hovering cloud onto the three white steps leading to a grand circular platform ahead. Her bare feet squeaked on the shiny, plastic surface. Once more she surveyed the saucer-shaped room. She narrowed her eyes against the glare from the bright, glowing white colours.

Directly in front of her was a large white egg-shaped seat. To her left were four more, smaller, egg-shaped chairs and the same to her right. The seats were all angled away from her line of sight and she couldn't see if they were currently occupied, but she had the feeling she was not alone. Beyond the seats, positioned from left to right, were five long, rectangular windows. The windows were completely blacked out although she was certain that once the shutters were opened she'd see a spectacular view into the world.

"If there is nothing else, I must tend to Percy and see to my masters," said Majordomo from the doorway. He bowed, turned and marched away.

The stone door slammed shut, casting a shadow across the room and caused a gust of air strong enough to disrupt the flow of three clouds, which moved backwards slightly before drifting forward again.

Xanadu was startled by an eerie, deep voice reverberating around the room. Her grubby hands began to shake.

"WHO DARES REQUEST AN AUDIENCE WITH THE COUNCIL OF ELDERS!" The voice demanded.

Quivering, she stepped into the middle of the platform and knelt on the white, glassy surface.

"Master, it is I, Xanadu, I have news."

An egg-shaped chair swung around on its axis. Xanadu raised her eyes and saw that it was sculpted to allow a comfortable seating position. A light within the seat flickered and an image of a green, crackling face appeared. As if it was a projection.

The deep wrinkles on the ancient face moved. "Council members, arise!"

Xanadu watched as one by one the chairs spun around in sequence and illuminated with a similar green light. All except one. The second seat to her left spun around, but it remained dark, entwined completely in thick dry cobwebs, as though it hadn't been used in centuries. The other projected faces became a blur and she beheld Lord Trident in front of her.

"Speak Xanadu! What news do you hold?" A collective grumble of voices chattered around her.

"Hear, hear!"

"Yes, speak up, Goblin."

"Why have you awoken us?"

"This had better be good!"

"Argh, awoken by a foul goblin!"

"Silence!" roared Lord Trident.

"My master," she said fumbling around in her dirty, yellow cloak and pulling out the blood red crystal, formerly worn by Lyreco and containing the soul of Trident.

"Lyreco is dead! Killed by the Gatekeeper."

"What?" Lord Trident thundered. Xanadu cowered, noticing that the room had suddenly become gloomy. The beautiful blue sky on the floor changed to a murky grey and the white clouds grumbled and moaned turning black and angry.

"Gatekeeper!" Trident demanded, closing his eyes. "Gatekeeperrrrr!" His fury echoed across the hollow room.

Without warning a purple gateway appeared, buzzing with electricity. The Gatekeeper shot through the Gateway and crashed onto the shiny floor. Snarling, he stood up and spoke, showing his yellow cracked teeth. "You summoned me, Lord Trident?"

"Do you no longer bow to your masters?" roared Lord Trident. The Gatekeeper's legs collapsed under him and he was forcefully held in place by an invisible hand.

"Why did you kill my servant?" Lord Trident demanded.

Struggling against the grip the Gatekeeper gasped, "You know why! He should have died centuries ago and the world was unbalanced. I took his brother to take his place but he … escaped my prison."

"You lie!" Trident shouted.

The Gatekeeper flinched, and the invisible hand clenched around his body squeezed, crunching and grinding his bones.

"When we made this world, you set the rule that all who die would become your eternal prisoners. No one can escape that jail, no one. I will ask you one last time! Why did you kill him?"

"Urrgh, because a life was taken that was not written. Bill Threepwood was killed when it was not his time and I've been blamed. Now your pet, Jimmy Threepwood has vowed to destroy me … the Keeper of Life and Death."

The invisible hand released its grip and the Gatekeeper fell to the floor.

"You fool. You know what happened last time with Argon. We knew he still cared for this world and that he has turned against us. It was my plan to have Bill Threepwood killed! To destroy any hope for Jimmy Threepwood. To turn him into the ultimate power, he must be fuelled by hate and revenge. Sadly, you will be his target. Now go! whilst I try and fix this mess, but remember what happened last time you failed me, Gatekeeper. Don't let it happen again!"

The Gatekeeper shuffled his feet and lowered his eyes. He turned to the cobweb covered chair and touched his disfigured face with the bony remnants of his hands. Memories flooded back. He glared at Xanadu and growled, "Be careful, Xanadu. If you weren't so important you would have met the same fate as Lyreco."

Slowly rising from the floor, clutching his cracked rib cage, the Gatekeeper formed a portal and escaped back into his unearthly prison.

"Rise, Xanadu," Trident whispered and the air once again became fresh and the sky returned to blue. "You have done well. But that fool has interrupted my plan. I need a replacement for Lyreco. Someone to wear the necklace containing my soul who will do my bidding … I've just the person in mind."

"Thank you, master, but I have more. Vesty has been located after all this time. He was hidden in the bell tower. He has captured Talula Airheart."

"Have no fear," the projected image said confidently. "I have no doubts about the power of the children of Tyranacus and I am sure this will come to a satisfactory conclusion. Now go. Make sure you place the necklace around the neck of …"

CHAPTER 22

Percy was dozing in his hospital bed. The world had drifted away, and he was caught in a memory.

Percy's Eleventh Birthday... The Timmins Household.

Percy was sitting up in bed surrounded by piles of brightly coloured wrapping paper. He felt empty and bored, so he grabbed the next present from the pile to his right, tore open the thin paper and crumpled it up, studied the present, then discarded it with the rest. Grabbing the next present like a conveyer belt worker, he muttered, "201," as he pulled off the tape.

There was a battle between his school classmates every year on birthdays and at Christmas over who would receive the most gifts. Percy couldn't even name ten of the presents he had received, it was all about the numbers and being able to brag to his friends the next day. He imagined the looks on their faces when he told them the final number, he couldn't wait. *No one will get near this number,* he thought, grinning.

He remembered his excitement the night before his birthday, how he jumped onto his bed and felt the butterflies in his stomach when he opened the first gift. That seemed like hours ago.

Giving a deep groan of boredom, he pushed a mountain of paper aside and picked up a red sealed envelope. He tore it open, dropped the envelope, slid out the card and immediately opened it flat, in anticipation of money falling out. Percy crooked his neck to see if it had gotten stuck. It was empty! He flung the card across his bedroom without bothering to check who it was from. The card flipped open and Percy saw two large yellow number Ones on the page with *Happy Birthday* written across the middle in yellow italics.

He contemplated his room. The sunlight was shining through the grand windows, illuminating the wooden floor and bouncing off the pinball machine, Olympic-sized trampoline and 60-inch television stuck high on the wall.

Irritated and bored he kicked his toys out of the way and pulled open the door. His feet sank into the luxurious carpet and his leaving indentations as he walked. Smiling to himself he saw one of the maids, a young nervous girl who had started working as a servant a few days before. The maid was walking towards him carrying a large silver platter containing his breakfast. With a smile he approached her. "Why, thank you very much Carrie, how very kind of you," he said, bowing.

Curtseying, her face came alive with happiness. "Morning, Percy, I've brought your breakfast."

Percy reached out to grab the tray and as their hands touched Carrie let go, instantly followed by Percy removing his hands. The clatter could be heard in the kitchen. The food and drink soaked into the carpet and the teapot bounced across the landing. Carrie stopped breathing when it burst through the wooden railings and plummeted to the grand foyer below. Percy watched hot tea splashing all over the wooden floors and turned back to Carrie, who was frozen. The antique silver tea pot exploded on the floor never to be used again. This job meant everything to her and Percy knew this was the end for Carrie.

Percy walked off smirking; the sound of Carrie's sobbing ringing in his ears.

He ran his hands down the bannister, admiring his family's wealth; the chandeliers clinging to the soaring ceilings, glorious expensive pictures spread across the walls; even the banister was made of gold, or so he liked to brag to his friends.

He whistled with pride and walked into the living room. Upon seeing his mother Percy said, "Anne, I seem to be light on the present numbers this year," he opened and closed his fists in a greedy fashion.

"Ah, darling," said Percy's mother, a pleasant woman with pronounced cheekbones and brown eyes. She was wearing an expensive lemon coloured dress. She produced three large presents each meticulously wrapped in bright red paper and tied with green silk ribbon.

"These are from Aunty Joan: and don't call me Anne! I'm your mother."

Percy snatched the presents and sat on the floor in front of the fire, muttering his disapproval under his breath.

He tore open the first wrapping but heard his father talking to his mother and the word 'present.' At once he lost interest in the gift before him, and stopped to listen. Through the corner of his eye he saw his father, a short overweight man with a flourishing curly moustache and a pipe protruding from his mouth.

"Yes, Anne, I'm not sure I like the current situation either. I agree that this house is far too small."

Anne's brown eyes glowed with delight. "Can we look tomorrow? This house is getting a little shabby."

Percy thought he heard a hissing noise from the present but ignored it, continuing to listen to his parents so he didn't miss a thing. The hissing started again and turning angrily at being distracted, Percy jumped and scrambled away from the present and onto a nearby chair. To his amazement the ribbon on his present had turned into a snake. His body trembled with fear as a vicious, thin green snake hissed and flicked its long pink tongue.

The other ribbons moved too and then burst into life as another two snakes grew, both flicking their tongues at Percy. Percy burrowed further and further into the chair, desperate to get away from the venomous serpents. He kept one eye on the reptiles and looked at his mother and father still engrossed in their conversation.

"Mum! ... Dad!" he whispered.

"Not now, Percy!" his father said, coughing into his pipe.

The first snake lunged forward at Percy snapping its fangs. Diving to the right Percy saw its teeth sink into the white leather as dirty yellow fluid dripped out of its mouth. Dodging again, this time to the left, the second snake struck. Its teeth became stuck in the leather and it wriggled to break free.

Hearing his mum and dad still talking and seizing his chance to escape, Percy tried to get up but was unbalanced and fell backwards into the chair. Before he had chance to move the third snake attacked, sinking its teeth deep into Percy's right wrist. It happened so quickly that Percy didn't feel any pain, just the build-up of pressure as the venom injected into his arm.

Screaming, he jumped from the chair and ran towards the kitchen. The snake released its grip and fell to the floor.

Anne and Percy's father stopped, stared at each other and Percy's father ran after Percy.

Percy's father got into the kitchen just as a maid had finished rinsing Percy's arm under chilly water and was wrapping a bandage around it.

"What, what is it boy?" he asked, stumbling over his words, his chin wobbling like a walrus.

A tearful Percy turned, struggling to breathe through the excitement and gasping for air, "A, a, a (*sniff*) snake, bit me! There were three of them in the presents and one bit me!" he said, talking extremely fast so that his father only caught the words snake and present.

"Snake!" he shouted, pulling the pipe from his mouth. He peered through the kitchen door into the lounge, staring at the pile of torn paper and ribbon.

He cleared his throat and stuffed the pipe into his trousers before creeping into the room quietly. He approached his wife. "Shhhh," he said, lifting a large finger up to his lips and pointing towards the paper. "Snake," he mimed.

"Snake!" Anne shouted, leaping up onto the chair as her eyes darted in every direction at once, scanning the room.

Barry Timmins gave a fierce, brave look of 'I'm not scared' to his son. Hesitantly he stretched out his left leg and used his slippered foot to stamp around the area by the fire. He kicked, but nothing, just bright red paper and thin strips of green silk ribbon.

Shrugging he went back to Percy, who had come into the lounge from the kitchen, to check his arm. He unwound the bandage and saw the two puncture holes piercing the skin. He held out his arm and his parents watched in amazement as the venom crawled under his skin like a parasite forming the shape of a 6.

At that very second the room, then the house started to shake. An expression of dread crept over Percy's father's face and Percy could see the same in his mother's eyes.

Re-bandaging his son's wrist as quickly as possible, Percy's father said, "Percy, go and play in the garden." His voice was quivering.

"But …."

"No buts, Percy, please go out. Your mother and I need to talk."

As soon as the door closed, Barry shut the blinds, ran to Anne and held her as tightly as he could.

CHAPTER 23

An expensive vase fell from the cabinet. Percy's mother and father watched, motionless. A deathly figure materialised in front of them.

The deathlike abomination, known as the Gatekeeper, stared at the Timmins through empty eyes, breathing deeply. Suddenly he stepped back and paced around the room like a caged animal.

"Arrgh, the Timmins family," said the Gatekeeper, and ran his nail through a yellow and brown piece of wrapping paper.

"You can't take him!" Anna said, and moved behind Barry's heavy frame to hide.

A menacing smile spread across the Gatekeeper's face. He glided forward and grabbed them both by the shoulders.

"You remember our deal, don't you?"

And with that, their grand stately home became transparent – the walls, the roof, everything, now as thin as paper. Then, it crashed down around them. They stood unharmed in the middle of where the house used to be looking on in horror. Before their eyes a shabby, run down house built brick by brick, began to grow out of the ruins around them. The windows were replaced by large wooden boards and a house a quarter of the size of the old one, appeared.

Anne's luxurious clothing shrank and tore, leaving only tattered rags. Other houses sprang up all around them in close proximity and images appeared of people walking in and out of their houses, putting washing on the line and sweeping up.

"No!" whispered Anne, burying her head in her husband's shoulder. "Not again, I can't go back to that … I can't, I won't."

"We made a deal eleven years ago and you were granted one wish. You asked for all the money in the world." The Gatekeeper's voice became crisp and menacing. "In return you agreed that on this day you would give your son to me, to be trained with others to rule this world. The only other condition was to make sure he had everything he ever wanted."

*   *   *

Percy was sitting in the garden. He picked up two large stones. Through the closed blinds he saw the silhouette of something, gliding smoothly around the lounge. He heard raised voices inside the house. He listened, and with his concentration elsewhere he suddenly felt a warm sensation in his hands. Staring down he saw a yellow, wavy fluid encasing the stones. The fluid hardened, and his hand dropped down through the sheer weight of the stones. The once rough, dirty rocks now felt as smooth as marble, yet as heavy as his 60-inch TV. Percy breathed in and whispered "Gold. I've turned stones into solid gold."

*   *   *

Percy opened his eyes. The dream about his eleventh birthday was fading in his mind. Taking a moment for his eyes to adjust, he saw he was in a medical room with a giant one-eyed ogre staring back at him. Harry and Jimmy were sitting either side of his bed. Grabbing the metal arm rests on the bed he pulled himself up but a sharp, burning pain jolted through his leg.

Wincing, he wiped his clammy head. Percy then noticed Xanadu standing next to the bed grinning uncomfortably with her teeth exposed.

"The piece of wood was not lodged in his leg too deeply," the ogre said, wiping his nose with his sleeve. "I've cleaned the wound." *This must be the nurse, and it operated on my leg with those dirty hands,* Percy thought. He was sure the others were thinking exactly the same thing.

"The problem," Nurse LaForte continued, "is that your bodies are decaying and rotting away. Look at the colour of the wound."

"It's black, look at it!" said Harry.

"It really smells!" moaned Jimmy, covering his nose with his robes.

"Hey!" shouted Percy, "This isn't a zoo!"

"His body is ravaged by evil magic and soon it will wither and die. All of you will wither and die."

Nurse LaForte faced Jimmy and Harry. "You must retrieve the Elixir and quickly."

"No!" shouted Jimmy. "First, we find Talula, and then we go after the flower."

"Don't be foolish, Jimmy!" shouted Xanadu the knee-high goblin, in her lizard-like voice. "By the time you save her it will be too late for all of you. Will you really risk destroying the prophecy for a girl?"

"Not just any girl," said Jimmy. "We need her to release Tyranacus."

"Jimmy, Xanadu is right. We need the Elixir, look at my leg. It could be you next."

Xanadu tried again. "I've heard rumblings that a band of misfits named the Light Dwellers are also seeking the potion."

Jimmy's heart skipped, and he studied his thumb nail. "They have somehow gained a map to find the Granite Fairies and they no doubt know the connection to the Palletine flower and its power. Should they find it first, all is lost."

"Harry? What do you think?" asked Jimmy.

"I say we rescue Talula first and then find the Elixir."

"That's two votes all," said Jimmy. "I have the scroll of the fairies and know their location, so I get the final say. We are going to save Talula first."

"But where do we start? They could be anywhere!" asked Percy.

"No," said Xanadu looking at LaForte. "I can show you Vesty's lair on the map."

"But how? Where?" asked Jimmy in surprise.

"Vesty was one of the children of Tyranacus, two millennia ago. After the purge, after his friend, his companion turned on him and became a traitor, Vesty changed. He left Lady Aurabella and the council and disappeared.

"We searched for him for hundreds of years, to …" she broke eye contact with the group and looked at the floor, mumbling, "… bring him back to the castle and give him his rightful place as ruler of the world. We found his lair, but it was empty. We had only just discovered his location when you ran into him."

The ogre wiped his nose and spoke again. "Before you attempt to find the lair you must seek out Typariio. She is a rather … special friend of mine; a witch doctor. She has a potion designed to slow the decay, and you will need it before you face Vesty."

CHAPTER 24

Harry stood up, almost toppling the small wooden raft as it drifted over the dead, black sea.

"Be careful!" shouted Percy, who was seated on the opposite side of the boat to Harry. "What arc you doing?" he asked.

"I wanted to try and see through this mist to where we are going!" replied Harry.

"Sit down," commanded Percy, "I don't want to be trying to find you in this water." He reached over the edge, drew up a handful of sludgy water and dropped it into the centre of the boat. It splattered on the floor. "I don't really want that stuff in my lungs. Do you?"

Harry did as he was told and sat back down, once again rocking the boat.

Jimmy felt the chilly air burrowing into his chest and pulled his robes tighter. For the past forty minutes all they'd seen was a wall of heavy fog and were now drifting into a foreboding narrow canyon of dense trees and overgrown shrubbery. He could feel eyes staring at him, and the presence of evil as noises from twisted creatures not of this world shrieked all around him.

"Hey!" said Harry, "did you see our guide? He's an old man who is completely blind. I say when we get to this house of Typariio we just get off without paying. What's he gonna do?"

A peculiar wind swept up the canyon, slicing through the blanket of fog and clearing the way in front of them. "I may be old and blind, young man, but I will assure you of one thing," the old man spoke with a deep, menacing tone. "This is the Passage of Demise. There is but one way in and one way out." The old man gave a maniacal laugh. "If you fail to pay me I will leave you at the House of Typariio and you will never find your way out. And that house is not somewhere you would wish to be for long."

Jimmy was seated at the rear of the boat directly opposite the guide, who was using two wooden oars and guiding them perfectly through the black sea. His face was wrinkled and leathery, his eyes cloudy blue as they peered through long greasy strands of hair falling over his face. When he smiled Jimmy noticed that the old man's black teeth pointed in random directions, reminding him of those on a jack-o'-lantern.

Jimmy wrapped his robes even tighter around his body and sat with his back to the damp, cold wood thinking about Talula trapped with that monster. Then he thought about his mother sitting in her house all alone. *Once this quest is over I'm going home to visit her for a few days. I need to make sure she's okay.*

Daydreaming, Jimmy hadn't noticed that the air had stopped whooshing around him and there was complete silence. No sound of the oars pushing through the water, no one breathing, nothing.

The sheet of fog parted, and a man appeared and clambered on to the boat. Despite his weight, the boat didn't rock as it had when Harry stood up. None of the other passengers appeared to notice this additional passenger, but Jimmy instantly recognised his face. "Mr Gibbs?" he asked. "But how …?"

The man stopped in front of Jimmy with his tiny glasses hanging off the end of his nose.

"Hello Jimmy, I'm glad you remember me. I cannot stay in this form for long, so I will be brief. I like you, Jimmy. I can see that you are special and destined for greatness. I like special people." He reached into a small pocket in his tweed waistcoat and pulled out a glistening round pocket watch, which he handed to Jimmy.

It felt heavy, but somehow warm. Jimmy turned it over and ran his finger over the engraving on the back. It read DOLT.

"Jimmy," Mr Gibbs said. "The time will come soon when you will need this watch. Remember. The watch is mightier than any sword."

The boat jolted, and Jimmy was rocked forward, and the fog suddenly lifted.

"We have arrived," the guide said, dropping his oars and thrusting his hand out for payment. Jimmy shoved the watch into his pocket before Harry or Percy could see it. He could feel the weight of it pulling the side of his robe down.

The children paid the guide and stepped off the boat. Shortly after, it drifted out of sight and the children stood alone in the cold, on top of a wooden ramp.

They stepped forward and a wave of intense, humid heat overwhelmed them. Harry pulled off his robe and held it in his hands. "What's happened?" he asked. "It's boiling hot."

Percy turned and walked back two steps, to where the air was still cold. "It's freezing over there, and boiling hot over here." He also pulled off his robe, draping it over his forearm.

A fist-sized dragonfly buzzed through the air and landed on Jimmy's nose. He swatted it and the dragonfly flew off, landing behind them on top of the thick black sea. The insect rested for a second, then began to flap its wings. As it took off, its leg got stuck in the thickness of the sea. Hovering only a few centimetres in the air and tugging with all its strength it pulled free from the sludge and awkwardly flew off.

Jimmy saw two glowing yellow eyes rising through the surface of the water, followed by another, and then another and three crocodiles emerged. They struggled through the tarry water and swam towards the bank below the children. The first crocodile clambered up the muddy bank and it opened its jaws, snapping aggressively towards them. The black water dripped off its body revealing tough, green scaly skin.

Jimmy was transfixed by the monster dragging its giant body up the bank with its tiny legs. Percy tugged his arm and pulled him into the undergrowth that surrounded the area. "Come on, Jimmy. I don't want to be around when those three reach the top."

Forcing his way through the heavy woodland, using his arms to push the giant plants and leaves aside, Jimmy felt the texture of the floor below him change. He felt the dusty, dry path become a spongy surface. He stepped into a mound of sloshy mud, which nearly tore his boot from his foot. He pushed a plant aside and crouched down.

"Here, it's a path, come on, we must be close," he said pressing forward.

They made their way through the small forest for another ten minutes.

"My mouth is so dry," said Percy, licking his lips. "I need water."

They finally burst out of the line of trees and were stopped in their tracks by the awe-inspiring view in front of them of vivid, beautifully designed and flowing gardens. All manner of flowers of assorted colours and sizes bloomed happily. Beyond the sea of gardens and colour stood a grand white mansion. It was completely out of place in the two micro climates they had just walked through.

Marble statues and expensive cars sat on a spacious driveway in front of the main doors.

"Look at those cars!" said Percy, pointing at the five cars parked outside the front door. "It looks just like my old house used to. Those were the days," he grumbled. "I was awoken each morning by maids bringing me breakfast and I had anything and everything I ever wanted."

A rumbling noise came from within the beautiful garden and water blasted high into the air from the sprinklers. Completely parched, Percy ran over the soft grass shouting, "Come on! Water!"

After drinking as much as they could and soaking their faces and hair, they approached the house with trepidation. Percy ran his fingers over the smoothly polished cars as he walked by them. The boys stepped under a huge stone archway and were ready to pull the dangling doorbell cord when the front door creaked open.

CHAPTER 25

Stepping into the cool, air-conditioned hall Harry couldn't see anything. It was pitch black and every window was sealed. "Hello!" he shouted, sending an echo through the house.

"Bubaballoo," a voice called out from behind the door. The group were startled and stepped back defensively, ready to strike.

A thin, gangly woman stepped out of the shadows. Her short wild hair sprouted out in every direction, giving her a Medusa-like appearance. Her face was as white as a ghost and she had black lipstick smeared all over her lips and around her eyes.

As she swung her long stringy arm forward Harry thought it appeared she didn't have a spine or bones and just floated along.

"Bubaballoo!" she shouted at the top of her lungs in a strong Caribbean accent. "I've been expecting you … Bubaballoo, Bubaballoo!"

The woman stepped back into the darkness and clapped her hands twice.

With a fizzle of electricity, the room burst into life. Trees and bushes were growing inside the house and they were teeming with bright lights and thousands of tiny yellow eyes. A waft of pungent swamp air filled the room. Multi-coloured mosquitos buzzed, and a shiny black scorpion scurried along the floor. A dozen slimy, poisonous toads hopped through the air and landed in the undergrowth.

"Bubaballoo to you all, which in my language means welcome, welcome all!" The woman beckoned the group forward.

Percy elbowed Jimmy and mouthed the word "snake," pointing at the female's black, skin-tight suit. Jimmy stared but couldn't see anything, just the type of a suit that a surfer would wear to keep warm.

"What?" he whispered back

Percy's face was filled with fright, Jimmy looked again and saw a green, hissing snake slithering around the woman's body and flicking its long pink tongue. "It's not real," he whispered. "Look, it's alive but somehow sewn into the clothing."

Both boys shifted their stares when the woman glared at them. With Jimmy's attention taken away from the snake the foul smell pulled at his stomach again and he saw where it was coming from. In the centre of the room was a swimming pool filled with thick smelly mud.

"Now, my children," she said. "I was told you were on your way."

Jimmy thought *by whom? I didn't see anyone.*

"I am Shango Typariio, world-renowned witch doctor and healer of all, especially your kind, yesss. Now, what do you think of my house? Not what you were expecting for a witch doctor, eh?" She nudged Percy with her pointed elbow, leaving a patch of sludge on his cloak.

"What do you think of the air conditioning? When I have guests, I turn the power on and the machine gives that horrid,

147

clean air smell. But now I know you are one of us you can feel the wonders of my house living all around you."

Shango Typariio sauntered to the mud bath in the middle of the room. It bubbled then popped, releasing a grey, oozing gas. She lowered herself into the swamp and swam to the middle, then ducked deep under the water.

Seconds later she burst back out and ran her long thin fingers through her hair. She got out, followed by a muddy crocodile, that toddled behind her leaving a trail of mud. Two bright yellow eyes flicked open and two mighty jaws opened wide to reveal razor sharp teeth before snapping shut. With a wriggle of its four stumpy legs the crocodile clambered up Shango Typariio's body and disappeared within her clothing.

"My family of crocodiles have brought me news. Three mystical warriors lost for centuries are currently travelling through one of my swamps in search of the Elixir."

Percy was surprised. "But how do you know about the Elixir?"

"Don't worry, young man. I know about you and what you seek. Your masters pay me well to look after you. I've dispatched some of my friends to ... slow them down. You need to hurry if you are to catch them and mmm, yes, free the fourth companion, isn't that right Jimmy Threepwood?"

All eyes turned to him as Jimmy felt a little uneasy.

"Yes, we all want to free Talula, don't we?"

"Come with me!" said Shango Typariio, pointing to the large kitchen to the right.

They went into the kitchen and the lights pinged on. Jimmy saw a wooden table in the middle of the room and two adjoining worktops. Each was brimming with jars containing insects and creatures, all filled to the top with brown, yellow and green water. Shango selected the first jar by the fridge, which contained a hand-sized centipede. She popped open the lid and discarded it on the floor.

"Come to Momma, my precious," she said and opened her mouth. The creature crawled in. Because her mouth was open, the boys saw it wriggling in her mouth before she closed her lips and swallowed. They watched on as the centipede reappeared, slipped out of her mouth and crawled down her body, around her black top and scuttled over the seemingly sleeping crocodile.

"Aah!" Shango said, licking her lips. "I thought she may have been in that jar too long and now she is whispering to me. Yes, far too long, Mama's sorry," she stroked her black top and the creature reacted by coiling its body.

Shango pulled open the fridge. The group were repulsed by the smell and the sight of food covered in green mould and wriggling maggots.

"Here it is," she said, pulling out a test tube filled with a pale sea green fluid. She lifted it up to the light and Jimmy could see little yellow bits floating around.

"Here, my children, each have a sip and you will feel replenished and as good as new."

"You go first, Harry," said Percy. "I don't want it first, what if it tastes gross, then no one else has it? What if it's some trick?"

Harry shook his head while Percy avoided his eye contact. Jimmy spoke, "We have to think of Talula, we don't have time for this. Here goes, even though I may regret it." Jimmy reached over, took the vial, pulled out the little cork and took a mouthful. Little lumps of fat and the slimy jelly fluid dripped down his throat. He covered his mouth to stop it coming back out. He burped. "It tastes like cheese mixed with cat food." He muttered.

Instantly his body felt rejuvenated. He examined his hands and saw that they'd changed back to his normal skin colour instead of the dirty blue they had been. Percy and Harry almost knocked him over in their rush to snatch the vial from his grasp.

Percy took a gulp and they all watched as the scar that had been left from the wound on his leg knitted back together. It turned bright pink before a layer of skin grew over the top.

"Remember, my children. This potion will only hold off the effects of your magic for a brief period. It will not be forever. For that you will need the flower … the Elixir. Now go! I have work to do." Shango Typariio grabbed a large kitchen knife from the table and thrust her face close to them speaking with malice, "Or you can stay with me and help with my … experiments."

CHAPTER 26

Higuain waded through the shin-high swamp and instinctively ducked as a bat darted over her head. She clutched the delicate scroll and tried to read the map whilst maintaining her balance. Dravid pushed forward and stopped at her shoulder. "What does it say? Are we on the right track?"

Tilting the map into the moonlight and running her eyes over the ancient text, Higuain nodded. "This is definitely the right way. Look, we passed those two mountains before we entered the swamp. This has to be right; come on, we need to keep going."

"Wait, we've been walking for hours. It's pitch black and cold. We need to rest, you're exhausted." Dravid said.

"We can't stop. We don't know how long Argon has left; we must find that potion, and fast," Higuain replied.

"It's okay, Higuain," Dravid said, grabbing her shoulder. "He's locked in the Eclipse portal. His body is frozen. No harm will come to him unless he is released. We must rest. You will be no good to anyone and we don't know what lies ahead."

The thought of Argon's face filled Higuain's mind. She wanted to carry on, she should carry on, but Dravid was right, she was no good to anyone exhausted. Dravid walked on, veering to the right into an opening leading into the forest.

The trees to the left rustled and moved, but Higuain couldn't see anything. A breeze stirred the forest. *I'm certain*

I saw someone. I need to rest, I'm seeing things, she told herself, running her hands through her hair.

In the middle of the forest, the group rested, Higuain clicked her fingers and sent a small flame to the floor, which set alight the pile of dry sticks Stratos had found. She swept her hair up into a pony tail and pulled off her soaking boots, placing them near the fire. She settled down with her back resting on a large tree stump.

"How did you meet him?" Dravid asked. "Argon, I mean."

It warmed Higuain's heart to think of him, of how she had been saved and a smile spread across her face.

"I was lost, a wandering soul and he saved me. He saved me in every sense. I am the last descendent of the Del Costa family. Since the beginning of time we were designated as guardians of the Knife of Arracni. It is a small blunt ceremonial weapon; the slightest swipe can tear a hole in the very fabric of time and space. The knife was given protectors, my ancestors. Once summoned by the Council of Elders they would lay down the weapon for the ritual and it would be used to release the mighty Tyranacus, thus starting the chain reaction that would end the world."

Flakes of burnt ash drifted into the air. "My family were forced into this life and were given no choice, but we were given special powers to protect the knife and stop it falling into the wrong hands. And there were many wrong hands that wanted it. The ritual continued for centuries, millennia even, and each time it became harder until shortly before the last purge, enough was enough. Sevra Del Costa took the weapon and went into hiding until I was born. He trained me in all the forms of combat and magic he knew and became my mentor according to the rules of the descendants. When I was old enough he passed the knife to me as its new protector and disappeared forever. What he had engrained in my mind from the moment I could walk was to hide the weapon at all costs, even if it meant sacrificing my own life to protect it and the world.

"Then they came for me …"

Many years ago …

Higuain gasped for air as she felt the icy water splashing her leg. She lost her footing and staggered, twisting her ankle. She stumbled to the forest floor for support. Dragging herself up she carried on, but each step sent a shock through her body. The rain dripped into her eyes blurring her vision. Higuain could feel her drenched clothes clinging to her body and the damp rubbing her skin but she staggered onwards again. Constantly checking the path from where she had come, she was breathing heavily. She was exhausted, and her legs were burning, but this was nothing compared to her ankle. Clenching the knife wrapped in a cloth tightly and pushing it under her cloak she thought, *this is the end for me, but I won't give this up, not without a fight.*

Higuain could hear the thunder of horses' hooves rumbling over the ground, and she imagined the sinister black winged horses snorting fire from their noses. She pushed aside a low branch and saw a small wooden shack in the distance. Higuain used the remainder of her energy to make it to the shack.

Slamming the wooden door shut she heard the horses screaming nearby. Her ankle gave way and she yelped, collapsing to the wooden floor. She dragged herself across the floor to a wooden table and chair positioned in the centre of the house.

Her heart was racing as she pulled herself into the shadows. *I need to rest, she thought, I need some strength. They're not going to end it like this.*

The door burst open, slamming into the wall. Dread overwhelmed her as four black shadowy robed figures glided in. The four warriors stood in a line in front of her shrouded in darkness and Higuain trembled in fear.

What are these things? She thought, fumbling behind her for somewhere to hide the knife. *Their eyes are burning red, that's all I can see, do they have faces?*

"What do you want!?" she screamed.

One of the spectral warriors stepped forward and said in a female voice, "You know what we are after, Higuain. Don't delay your demise any longer. We have been looking for you for a long time."

The female warrior stepped forward and flicked her gloved hand at the wooden table that was blocking her path; it flew through the air, smashed into the wall and exploded, leaving a gaping hole.

"The knife! Now!"

With her heart rate racing, strategies rushed through Higuain's head. *I must go for it; this may be my only opening.*

Higuain created a fireball in her hand and threw it with all her strength. The fireball tore through the air like a homing missile, but the hooded female raised her right hand and it fizzled into nothing on impact.

Before she could strike another fireball attack in her hand, Higuain was struck down by the female warrior's counter attack, which burnt her shoulder. Higuain had nothing left to give and slumped to the floor. The knife fell from her hand and skidded out of her reach. The warrior stepped forward and used her boot to push Higuain out of the way before securing the knife.

She turned elegantly and walked out of the shack with the final words, "Vesty, finish her: make it quick!"

"Yes, mistress Aurabella!" he replied sarcastically.

Through blurred vision Higuain saw the three warriors leave. One stayed, his eyes burning an intense, fiery red as a black whip snaked from within his right sleeve. When he cracked it on the floor it sounded like thunder rumbling in the heavens. The whip ignited, covered in vibrant electricity. Higuain could see her demise was near.

She closed her eyes waiting for the end, but heard a second voice. "Vesty! Let me deal with her. I need the practice. My aim has been a little rusty lately."

Vesty growled, "Make it quick, I have things to do."

The wooden door slammed shut and heavy boots stomped towards Higuain. She opened her eyes and saw the male's eyes change from demonic red to soft brown. He pulled back his cowl and Higuain saw a distinguished sculptured face and the image of an owl embroidered onto his robe.

"We don't have much time," he whispered. "Meet me tomorrow, here!" He shoved a piece of paper into her hand. "My name is Argon."

The strange man lifted the legless wooden table and placed it over her body. "Scream as loud as you can ... and don't be late."

Vesty saw the side of the shack implode as a bolt of light dragged the roof inwards and the building came crashing down. Argon sauntered out and climbed on his horse ...

*　　　*　　　*

"He saved me that day," said Higuain, her body suddenly feeling warmer and not so damp.

*　　　*　　　*

… Argon stood with his hood up in the centre of a market town; he spoke to Higuain with aggression.

"Why did you run with the knife? Why did you hide, tell me!"

Taken aback, Higuain stood ready to attack, flooded with emotion. "Because I'm sick of it! The destruction, the fear. Why would you want to destroy this world? So, to answer your question … I ran because I am not a monster!"

His face softened. He smiled and took her hand. "I was hoping that was the reason. I think we can help each other. I have a plan …"

*　　　*　　　*

"So that's it, and here I am. What about you, Dravid? How did you meet Argon?"

A look of remorse appeared on his face. "Urm, come on, we have rested enough. We need to keep going."

CHAPTER 27

The trio, Higuain, Dravid and Stratos, continued on their path and found themselves back in the shin-high swamp. Watching Dravid step through the water, Higuain saw it again, a blur of movement in the trees opposite. She grabbed Stratos' muscly arms and pointed. "Did you see that?"

"What?" moaned the man mountain.

"Never mind." *I'm certain I saw something. I must be tired.*

They trudged through the thick swamp for about an hour but Higuain couldn't shake the feeling of being watched, a sensation of imminent danger. All her senses were tingling as her training kicked in and her muscles tightened ready for anything.

Scrutinising the environment, she felt the temperature of the swamp below her feet slowly rising. A bubble appeared from the water and popped, followed by another, then another. The three warriors stood back to back with their weapons poised and they circled, gaining a clear view of their surroundings.

A raven squawked high in the trees overhead. The three were distracted and in that instant, six swamp hands shoved their way through the surface of the swamp. They grabbed the ankles of the three companions tightly and tried to drag them down.

Stratos pulled his axe from behind his back and struck down, cutting the hand in two. Higuain fashioned a ball of fire and released it, but it glanced off the surface and exploded, showering the air with mud.

Dravid immersed himself in the water and became one with it, allowing it to flow through him. Higuain could see it being pushed and pulled all around his body and organs as though it was blood being filtered and cleaned through century-old volcanic rocks.

"I'm always amazed by your healing power; it's so beautiful," she said, as his body glistened a sparkling light blue.

Dravid used his mind to control the fluid and the two hands clamped to his ankles released their hold and then the other hands holding Stratos and Higuain transformed into a waterfall and drained back into the swamp.

"What was that?" asked Stratos, wiping the mud from his face and flicking it back into the swamp.

"Must have been some sort of organism from within," said Dravid, his body slowly returning to normal. "Whilst it was under my control I could feel another presence controlling it, they were very strong …."

In mid-sentence Dravid began to shake uncontrollably. The purified water circling through his body became dirty brown and thickened, clogging the flow. Dravid started coughing violently. Stratos grabbed his shoulder.

"Look at his eyes, they're lifeless!" he cried.

The dirty brown swamp water oozed through Dravid's pores and solidified, creating a solid brown case of cement around him.

In a panic, Higuain grabbed Dravid's other shoulder. "What's happening to him?"

Before Stratos could respond, the mud on his face started moving, then transformed into the shape of a hand, which started squeezing his skull. Yelping in pain Stratos grabbed the hand with his giant fists, but eight more hands emerged from the swamp, locking around the three warriors' hands and feet. Just as it had with Dravid, the swamp and the hands dried out like cement and their bodies were imprisoned. Their feet were cemented in the water and their bodies secured like statues.

Even using all his brute strength, Stratos couldn't move. They were defenceless.

"It's okay, we can get out of this. We just need to remain calm," Higuaín murmured defiantly. The trees in front of her rustled and she was sure she'd seen something. "There it is again, I knew something was following us! What have you done to us!" Higuain shouted. "Show yourself, coward!" She tried to wriggle free. Whatever it was she'd seen, flashed past again. "Show yourself! Do your worst!"

The bushes parted, and a figure emerged from the bushes.

"Jimmy!" she said amazed. "Jimmy Threepwood!"

"Who?" shouted Stratos.

Higuain could see that Jimmy's skin was silvery and transparent and seemed to be flowing around his body. "What happened to you, Jimmy?"

Jimmy smiled. "I've been following you and your companions, the Light Dwellers, for a while, Higuain. I am not who you think I am. I do look like the boy you met and who gave you the map you possess. We are entirely different in many ways, yet we are also very alike. You see, the Jimmy you know has started down a path he is not ready to return from, a path of revenge, hate. Those negative emotions forced me to separate from his body."

"So, you are part of him?" asked Higuain.

"Yes, I am his goodness, his right and wrong, his love and compassion. Until we are reunited the world is in great peril. He is far more powerful than he, or anyone else realises and now his only concern is to destroy the Gatekeeper, at any cost."

"Can you help us?" she asked

"Yeah," shouted the giant Stratos. "Just free my axe and I'll smash my way out."

"Hold on," Translucent Jimmy said softly. He walked to Dravid and took a firm hold of his coarse stone head with both hands. He shut his eyes and concentrated. Silvery fluid drained from his body and flooded into Dravid's skin. As the lines of liquid penetrated, the cement cracked and bit by bit crumbled to the floor. Higuain watched and could see the water in Dravid's body changing. It pumped the dirty water around until it was purified. With a deep gasp Dravid opened his eyes, an aura of intense silver light shimmering around him.

Surrounded by the light, the boy morphed into a small silver phoenix, gracefully flew high into the air before plummeting downwards like a missile and smashing through the top layer of cement.

The warriors struggled to retain their balance as the ground below them rumbled and shook. Cracks streamed across the surface, which then split and separated. The cement crumbled and become fluid once more, turning back into the thick, watery mud. The group struggled out of the mud and staggered back onto dry land. They dragged their boots on the ground to wipe off the excess mud. Once they had calmed down they stared at Jimmy who was still shimmering. With a graceful smile and a nod Jimmy turned and walked away.

"Wait!" Higuain shouted. "Where will you go? What will you do?"

Translucent Jimmy carried on without looking back.

"Join us!" shouted Higuain. "We know you were following us. I can see in your eyes that you want to help, at least to re-unite with Jimmy."

Translucent Jimmy slowed but still didn't turn. "But what happens if we have to fight them? If he destroys me, that will be the end for everyone. I am the only one who can bring him back to the light."

Higuain approached him and on taking his hand she felt a surge of warmth and love flow through her blood. She hadn't felt that sensation since she last saw Argon.

"Let's worry about that, then," she pulled him back to the group.

"What's your name?"

"I, I don't really have one," said the boy. "I never needed one before."

Higuain pointed at the perfect silvery light being cast from his body onto the forest ground. "Shimmer, we'll call you Shimmer. Shimmer, let me introduce you to Stratos and of course Dravid."

CHAPTER 28

Jimmy soared through the air, but the paper scroll he was holding flapped over and nearly tore from his hand. The fast air flooded his lungs and he lost his breath. Jimmy panicked and thrust his head into the neck of the huge yellow and blue dragon he was riding, feeling the rough, jagged scales on his cheek. He consulted the scroll once again.

"There," he shouted, pointing down to a lively, bustling city shopping centre.

Percy, who had earlier transformed into the mighty dragon, arched and let out a holler. He swooped down casting a shadow over the area.

Jimmy felt Harry's hands tighten around his waist.

"How are we going to land and not be seen? And why are we both riding this beast? You could have flown here yourself."

Percy angled his body for the descent and Jimmy gripped the reins tighter, the blood draining from his hands. Through fear he shouted, "I wish I had flown myself now, but because I …" He gritted his teeth as the ground got closer and closer. Percy was making no attempt to slow down. "But because I didn't want two of us to be exhausted because we don't know what we'll facccccee …."

Percy circled then opened his remarkable wingspan and braked suddenly before landing in one of the empty back alleyways. On landing his talons caught on three tin dustbin cans sending them flying through the air. A cat darted to safety.

Morphing back into human form Percy collapsed, and Harry only just caught him before he hit the cobbled floor.

"Come on!" shouted Jimmy eager to keep moving.

"Wait, Jimmy. Look at him, he's exhausted. Give him a second to rest," pleaded Harry.

"Harry, we don't have a second. A second is all Talula may have. Let's at least find the Lair and I'll go in ... alone. Then you can follow when Percy is better."

Harry shook his head, pulled Percy's arm around his shoulder and helped him out of the alleyway.

Jimmy glanced over at Harry dragging Percy along, but hurried on ahead too busy thinking about what that monster had done to Talula to notice the end of the alley. He bumped straight into a woman with her hands full of her shopping. She was pulling a small boy, who couldn't have been more than four or five, behind her.

Upon impact the woman staggered, dropping bags full of designer clothes onto the dirty ground.

"Hey! Watch where you're going!" she yelled and bent down to collect her bags.

"I'm sorry," Jimmy mumbled sheepishly, and he tried to help her.

"I've got them!" the woman replied, tut-tutting through her bright red lipstick. She stalked off with her high heels clopping along the cobblestones.

The little boy turned back. He stared at Jimmy with a V-shaped frown and it felt as though his eyes were piercing Jimmy's very soul.

"Don't do it!" whispered the little boy. "Don't destroy the world."

The woman yanked the little boy's arm and pulled him away from Jimmy and his friends.

Did that boy really say that? Was I dreaming it? Jimmy wondered.

Jimmy was still staring at the boy and his mother as they continued and were lost in the crowd. Harry and Percy staggered up behind him.

"Come on Jimmy. I thought you were in a rush!" shouted Harry, panting from the strain of helping Percy. Jimmy was still staring into the hordes of people; his mind wondering about the future.

"I'm coming …."

Jimmy took the scroll out of his cloak once more and studied it, then paused and scanned the hundreds of people walking past focusing on their own lives. They had no idea of the future or the events prophesied. He remembered the stories Lyreco had told them of how the world would be destroyed, and he looked at the crowds rushing around like bees collecting nectar and he pitied them. *I wonder what they would do if I told them what was coming? Would it change their lives, or would they be better off not knowing? I bet they wouldn't believe me anyway.*

He set off once again and passed a telephone kiosk, tall stone walls and all manner of shops and market stalls spread out as far as the eye could see. He saw a chemist, and then a clothes shop, his attention captured by a grubby man with a shabby black beard, standing behind a fruit and vegetable stall shouting, "A pound for my best strawberries. A pound for today, come and get them! Just a pound." The man noticed Jimmy staring and seized his chance. "Have ye had your five of the day, ma boy?" he shouted. "How about an arple or a nice perrr?" Jimmy shook his head, broke eye contact and walked on until he was clear of the man.

Jimmy walked six more steps, whilst holding the tattered yellowy paper in front of his face. He stopped.

"This is it!" he said thrusting his finger into the scroll. "This is the exact spot Xanadu circled as Vesty's lair."

"I don't see anything," said Harry.

"Nor do I," said Percy. "Nothing but shops, Jimmy. You sure this is the right place?"

Jimmy walked over to a bright red post box and tapped it with his knuckle, but nothing happened. He rested his back on the post box, and scrutinised the scroll again, rubbing his fingers over some lines that had formed on the page.

"This has to be it!" he said to himself. "It has to be here somewhere."

Opposite the post box was a sweet shop with a large bay window a metre off the floor and a vast array of tantalising sweets on display. The shop had been painted bright pink and the sign read, 'Pocket Penny Sweets Ltd.'

Harry helped Percy and braced him against the wall next to the shop window leaving him to rest since he was still visibly drained.

"Where is it?" Jimmy shouted, and a host of shoppers glared at him as they walked past.

"Xanadu said it was right here." He said, jabbing the paper with his finger. He could feel the pressure building up. The beast within him was bubbling and getting angry. "Arrgh!!" He shouted and kicked a tin can.

"Calm down, Jimmy," said Harry with authority. "We'll find her; the lair must be here somewhere."

Percy started to regain focus. He pointed at the mouth-watering sweets beckoning from the window, and licked his lips. Delirious, he stumbled forward, rubbing his shoulder against the brick work and stretching out his hand.

"Harry, help Percy, he's going to fall!" said Jimmy. A bell jingled and the door to the sweet shop swung open. A little grey-haired man wearing a red striped apron and carrying an old straw brush came out thrashing it wildly through the air.

"You lot again!" The man said and jabbed at Jimmy and Harry. "I'm sick of you lot hanging about my shop."

Jimmy and Harry pointed at their chests. "What, us?"

"Yes, you lot!" the man said and hit Jimmy on the shoulder. "You stand there in your creepy robes then disappear. Go on, shoo, shoo, it's bad for my custom and people think I am mad, but I know what's going on. Bill Drake has put you up to this! He's been after my shop for years." The old man's voice turned to a shout. "But you tell him from me, he ain't getting it."

"Okay, okay," said Harry "We'll move!" and whispered "Crazy old man." Out of the corner of his eye, Jimmy watched Percy who was still stumbling around. He tripped and fell body first into the large shop window. In a blink he was gone, disappeared into nothing.

Jimmy smiled and took a deep breath. "Come on Harry, Percy has figured it out. I know where the lair is hidden."

CHAPTER 29

Harry and Jimmy waited for a group of school children who were jostling and giggling while entering the shop, hoping they'd distract the crazy shopkeeper.

"Now!" Harry shouted, and the pair ran back to the spot where Percy had disappeared only moments earlier. Harry reached out and touched the bay window and his hand disappeared. A faint voice echoed all around them, sounding as though it was from the other end of the street.

"Hellowww! Harry? Jimmy is that you? I'm down here, in the window. Help me!"

"Percy!" yelled Harry, before climbing through the window and jumping into the unknown. Jimmy quickly followed.

"Percy, are you okay?" said Harry, picking himself up from the floor.

"Urgh!" shouted Jimmy from high above, followed by a crash as he clattered on top of Harry. They eventually disentangled themselves and stood up.

The cold, decayed air hit Jimmy. The foul smell of sewers and death forced its way into his throat and tugging at his oesophagus. Jimmy grimaced when he saw that he was covered in a sticky, moist slime. "What is this stuff?" he asked, sniffing it.

Droplets of dirty water fell and dripped on the boys' faces, then plopped into the ankle-deep puddles of water that surrounded them. Jimmy inspected the gloomy green walls of the damp cylindrical hallway in front of them.

"It's some kind of sewer running under the town," he said, creating a flame in his hand so he could see. The flame swirled around his hand but as it touched the remnants of slime between his fingers it exploded into the air in a cloud of fire.

"Whoa!" shouted Jimmy, patting the flame out on his smouldering robes. "This sticky stuff is really flammable. We'll need to be careful."

Jimmy made sure he'd wiped off all the slime before he illuminated his hand once again, and held it high in the air. The flame danced, then dimmed, extinguished due to the lack of oxygen. By moving the flame around, he could see that the walls were coated in the oozing slime. Large droplets of water echoed around the cesspit like a dripping tap plopping in the dead of night.

Jimmy spotted Percy, who was wobbling about on unsteady legs. He helped him regain his balance.

"I'm feeling better, although my legs aren't helping," said Percy.

Jimmy stepped forward into the darkness but something hard crunched below his foot and rolled sideways, crashing against the wall. Jimmy bent down and held up the light. To his surprise he saw that the path ahead was littered with every variety of human bones. The cracked skull he had stepped on had rolled against the wall and was propped against an old rusted sword and a red circular shield.

"Looks like we aren't the first to find this place," said Percy sloshing, through the water.

"Let's just hope we're the last!" replied Jimmy, heading into the gloomy cylinder ahead.

They walked down five long twisting corridors. Percy stopped. "Look, a light over there!"

"Shhh!" whispered Harry, putting his fingers to his lips. Jimmy nodded and extinguished the flame in his hand. They crouched down, disappearing into the shadows

They crept slowly towards the light and suddenly the tunnel opened out into a room. At one end they could make out what seemed to be steps leading downwards.

Jimmy whispered, "I'm going to crawl over there to see what's below, okay? Keep quiet."

He edged forward and saw about thirty steep steps leading down at a ninety-degree angle into the base of a chamber below. Jimmy peered over the edge. The sheer drop made him grab the edge tightly. Plumes of steam jettisoned from vents all over the floor clouding the air every few seconds. As it dispersed Jimmy could see piles of bones dotted around a giant square in the middle of the room with rats gnawing on any remaining flesh, squeaking in delight.

As the curtain of steam lifted, he saw two huge golden chairs, one slightly taller than the other. In the taller chair sat the winged, pig-faced abomination, black wings tucked behind him and the flute in a stand next to him. On his head was a crown covered in glistening jewels, and draped over the back of the throne was a perfect red and white robe befitting royalty. And there, next to Vesty, was Talula, and it was clear that she was completely under his spell locked in a state of mid-transfer to her inner bat creature.

Sliding back into the shadows Jimmy whispered, "Vesty is down there, dressed as some sort of king."

"With Talula?" asked Harry

"Yeah, she's with him and seems to be completely under his spell."

"What's the plan?" asked Percy, "what are we going to do?"

"Plan?" whispered Harry. "We don't need a plan. There are two of them and three of us."

"But we can't hurt Talula."

Harry stood up and walked into the room and stopped above the steps, in full view of those in the chamber at the bottom.

"Harry!" shouted Jimmy, but it was too late. They had been seen.

Percy yanked at Jimmy's sleeve and they both followed Harry. They didn't have much choice.

Seeing a flash of movement above him, Vesty raised his eyes. He snarled in surprise but didn't move from his seat. "How did you find this place?" he roared.

"Just give us Talula—in her normal form—and we'll be on our way. You don't have to die here, Vesty," said Harry defiantly.

Smiling, revealing his pig-like fangs, Vesty spat out his words. "I can't do that, I'm afraid."

The three boys moved cautiously down the steps into the grand chamber, focused completely on Vesty and Talula. They reached the bottom of the steps.

Suddenly Percy shouted, "I see you like gold and jewels? Let her go and I can create a room full of it just for you."

Percy picked up a stone from the floor and concentrated hard. The stone in his hands crackled and turned to gold. The precious metal then spread all over the section of wall next to where he was standing.

"Fools!" Vesty shouted. "I don't wear the crown and robes because I like gold. I wear them because I like to see what I will look like when I am the ruler of this world. I will fashion the next design of humans in my image. You and your meddling have already affected my plans. When you are destroyed, and the time is right, we will open the portal and end this pathetic, weak world. I've waited a long time for this. I already know the location of the knife of Arracni to tear open the fabric of reality and I know who the key is." Vesty laughed victoriously. "Once Talula and I have possession of the knife we will force the key to help us perform the ritual, and the beast will be ours."

"Key? What key?" said Jimmy. "What are you talking about? You need all four of us to open the realm."

"You poor pathetic children. So many lies. You are not needed to release the beast. You are needed to *control* it! The Elders created you, so once the beast has been released, the four of you combined have the power to command the beast and prevent it killing the Elders.

"Two millennia ago, when Argon turned on us and left us, we were almost able to control the beast between the three of us. It was hard because the beast turned on us many times, one of those times it nearly killed Aurabella. It tried to destroy the council, but we held together and survived."

"But you won't have the four of us to help you. How will you control it? With only Talula?" Harry demanded.

Laughing, Vesty snarled. "That is the difference. I've no intention of controlling it. Once released, Tyranacus will destroy this world and the council leaving me and ... Enough of that. I've told you too much already."

Vesty grabbed the flute and played a few notes. Talula sprang from the throne, a web of saliva dripping from the corners of her mouth.

"I wonder how old you are?" Vesty asked. "I wonder if you have been taught the power of re-animation yet?"

Narrowing his eyes and focusing, he commanded "Abberrennnto!"

Behind them, an orchestra of groans echoed through the cavern and up into the tunnels, followed by a procession of footsteps marching toward them in perfect unison. The human bones had come to life.

Jimmy's eyes were drawn to the stone square in front of Vesty. The piles of crumbling bones moved, pulled away from the rats, which scampered away. The bones seemed to be being dragged along the floor by an invisible force. The bones clicked back into their sockets and four animated skeletons stood up, wobbling on their new feet, and marched to an arsenal of weapons hanging on the nearby wall.

The boys could hear a cacophony of footsteps above them being amplified through the narrow corridor and it sounded like rolling thunder coming closer and closer. The group backed tightly against the wall looking at the four-armed skeletons stumbling towards them.

A skeleton appeared from the tunnels above grimacing, scraped his rusted sword on the wall and raised his shield in wrath.

"You two take the ones from the tunnel. I'll take these here," yelled Harry.

Before either Jimmy or Percy had time to protest, Harry was already charging towards the skeletons, sending a stream of red light at the first warrior. Seeing the beam too late the skeleton warrior raised its shield, but the blast was too fast and too powerful. The beam hit the angled shield and deflected upward, punching the bony skull clean off its neck and sending it sliding across the floor towards Vesty's feet. The warrior continued moving onwards, headless. Harry let loose another beam using his right hand. The warrior batted it away with its shield, leaving its body exposed. Harry fired a second beam with his left hand hitting the skeleton square in the chest, and as it erupted, shards of bone crumbled to the floor.

High above Percy, the lead skeleton, followed by four others, awkwardly walked down the steps, their bony legs wobbling as if they belonged to someone else. With the sword in its right hand, it scraped the eroded metal along the wall creating small sparks which spurted into the air. The warrior reached the step above Percy and thrust its lifeless arm across its chest before striking towards the head of its target. Percy ducked out of the way and the sword smashed into the wall, sending a ripple of vibration up the skeleton's arm. Percy created a ball of fire and unleashed it into the skeleton's unguarded abdomen.

The force of the blast sent the warrior hurtling backwards. It crashed into the other skeleton warriors behind it and they all clattered onto the floor. Behind Percy a lightning bolt formed in Jimmy's hands and he threw it at a group of skeletons who had appeared from the tunnel above. The lightning bolt soared over the heads of the skeletons and imbedded in the wall. Instantly the sparks from the lightning ignited the green sludge on the wall as the whole tunnel erupted in fire causing the whole cavern to shake violently.

Jimmy looked down to Harry and nodded in admiration at the two piles of singed, smouldering bones near his feet. Harry was being circled by the last two warriors, who were jabbing at him with their swords and using their shields to fend off his attacks.

"Come on!" shouted Percy, brimming with adrenaline, and rushed past Jimmy to help his friend.

Jimmy was about to charge after Percy when out of the corner of his eye he looked towards Vesty. Jimmy saw that his eyes were closed and that he was twitching and looked like he was in a deep trance. *Re-animation magic, I remember doing it.* Jimmy thought. *If I lost my focus the creatures collapsed.* Generating a javelin of lightning in his right hand he aimed at Vesty, then threw it with all his might. Vesty was focusing so hard he had no idea what was coming. Percy and Harry watched as the bolt screamed through the air.

CHAPTER 30

Talula pounced, swatting the lightning bolt with her razor-sharp claws as if it was a fly. The projectile bounced twice on the floor and sizzled out. Vesty opened his eyes at the commotion breaking the spell, and the two remaining skeletons crumpled to the floor.

Vesty stood up, removed his crown, carefully placing it on the throne and stepped onto the stone floor.

"You may be able to beat a few worthless skeleton warriors, but can you defeat one of your own?" Vesty pursed his lips and lifted the flute to his mouth. The music bounced around the acoustic chamber. Talula roared and stamped her feet. Her robes were shredded, hanging on her like pieces of rag. Snarling, the hairs covering her body stood on end and Jimmy could see that the real Talula was gone. He knew she was in there somewhere, but this beast wasn't her.

Talula bounded forward on her hind legs. Percy's hand burst into fireballs but Harry grabbed his sleeve.

"I've got an idea, but you'll need to protect me," he said, focusing on Talula. Harry sidestepped into the shadows of the staircase and stood underneath the deathly drop where they first entered the room.

He took a deep breath and his eyes became the colour of the moon.

"Nierro, Nierro!" Harry shouted, and his voice became distant, forceful, as a gust of air ruffled his robes.

The ground below his feet rumbled and a giant lizard burst through the stone floor, leaving a pile of broken slabs and dust. Its long, armoured tail thrashed behind it and holding its clawed hands out, it leapt forward and crashed into Talula. They collided, and rolled forward smashing into the throne and obliterating it. Talula staggered to her feet and slashed out with her claws, catching the lizard on the face. The lizard gave a high-pitched shriek in anger. It retaliated by slashing its tail and swiping her legs out from under her, before diving on top of her pinning her to the ground.

"We need to help Harry," shouted Percy, "he needs to concentrate. Do you think the two of us can take Vesty?"

Jimmy's eyes blazed fiery red and the monster inside him bubbled to the surface. "For what he did to Talula I will handle him on my own."

Vesty's wings unfurled and he tucked the flute into his waist belt. A black leather snake-like whip slithered out of his cloak and as it touched the floor it snapped into life channelling electricity. Scowling, Vesty stepped forward huffing and grunting. With a flick of his wrist, the whip lashed through the air catching Percy on the left shoulder and tearing his cloak. Percy grabbed the wound and warm blood trickled through his fingers.

Percy cast a ball of fire and threw it at Vesty, who simply batted it away with his left hand. Fury filled Percy's eyes and he charged towards the wing monster. Vesty leapt high into the air flapping his wings, and once more unleashed the whip, wrapping it around Percy's chest and sending a thousand volts through his body. Percy was flung across the room and smashed into the solid wall. Vesty landed, raised the whip and cracked it again, this time hitting the base of a stone pillar supporting the ceiling in the corner of the room. Percy opened his eyes as the giant pillar, followed by some of the ceiling, tumbled towards him. With the last of his strength he released a jet of fire, which knitted the rock together, but still they crashed down on top of him and he fell silent. A plume of smoke filled the air.

"Percy!" Jimmy screamed. He felt rage welling up and the aura of green flame enveloped his body.

"You will pay for that!"

Smiling, Vesty whipped the floor and nodded.

Before Jimmy had time to react, the charged whip lashed at his face, connecting with a stone slab behind him. The slab split down the middle and crumbled to the floor. Jimmy glared at Vesty and clenched his fist, creating two lightning bolts. Instead of throwing them he held them like swords, glistening and hissing in his hands.

Vesty saw his chance as Talula was thrown and crashed into the wall next to him. Vesty closed his eyes and the bones behind Harry once more combined and clambered to their feet. Harry was defenceless against the staggering skeleton. It approached from behind and hit Harry over the head with a shield and he crumpled to the floor. Picking up a nearby sword the warrior thrust it to Harry's chest pinning him to the ground.

With Harry's concentration broken, the giant lizard groaned, before being sucked back into the earth. Talula dug her nails into the ground, pulled herself up and despite her injuries followed Vesty.

"You have lost, Jimmy Threepwood and your band of misfits. You would have been no match for me, Aurabella and the others. No match at all," declared Vesty.

Jimmy looked around the chamber. Talula, locked in her beast form was limping away. Percy was crushed under a mountain of rubble and Harry was at the mercy of a skeleton warrior. *All is lost,* Jimmy thought, *I can't win on my own ... No! I must win. I will beat him!* He stared at the flute tucked into Vesty's belt. Jimmy could see Harry was starting to stir and come around.

"Enough of this!" Vesty shouted, pulling the whip back over his shoulder, ready to use again. Slashing forward with all the strength he could muster Vesty unleashed his whip. Jimmy lifted the lightning sword in his left hand and the weapons entangled, sending a blaze of electricity into the air.

Vesty's speed had caused him to lose his balance. Jimmy yanked the sword, pulling the whip and Vesty towards him. With a sharp kick, the flute flew from Vesty's belt and spun high into the air.

"Now, Harry! Now!" Jimmy screamed.

Before the skeleton warrior could react, Harry channelled a beam of energy into its rib cage and it exploded in a blaze of light, showering Harry in bone fragments. With the mystical flute spinning through the air, he released a final stream of power from his right palm and hit the flute. The flute snapped into two pieces and fell to the stone floor. Harry's strength was drained, and his body surrendered. He slumped down unconscious.

Talula screamed loudly, held her head and dropped to her knees before collapsing.

Vesty thrashed his claws and knocked the second lightning sword from Jimmy's hand. On the return swing he caught him hard in the face, leaving three deep claw marks. Reeling away Jimmy tried to create a counter-attack but Vesty kicked him in the chest and he crumpled to the floor. Vesty leapt on top of him and raised his claw high above his head.

"You have caused me a lot of problems, Jimmy, but no more!"

Jimmy turned his head and once again saw Harry injured and helpless. He saw Vesty's claw with its dirty nails sparkling in the light. Memories raced from the depths of his mind as the claw lowered towards him.

An instant before he was struck, a jagged weapon plunged through Vesty's stomach. Spots of blue blood dripped on to Jimmy's chest. Vesty stopped short, jerked, twitched and stared down at his stomach. In the centre of the wound were the sharp edges of the snapped flute.

Exhausted from what she had done, Talula collapsed to the floor. Vesty slumped on top of Jimmy with his claws wrapped tightly around the flute. Blood trickled down the side of Vesty's mouth and he slurred his final words,

"There is another, Jimmy Threepwood!" He gave a weak laugh. "There is another!" and fell to Jimmy's side.

Jimmy rushed over to the barely conscious Talula. He pulled her up and helped her to the steps before grabbing Harry's arm and shaking him.

"Harry, come on, I need your help, wake up."

Jimmy began removing rocks from the top of a mound in the corner. He was exhausted, and his arms were weak, but he used every bit of his energy to help Percy.

Pulling off the last stone, Jimmy was astonished to see a flat blanket of smooth, warm rock. He slid it off and found Percy underneath, covered in cuts and grazes but okay. Jimmy helped Percy up, and he dusted himself off.

"I melted the rocks, it took everything I had but it created some sort of shield."

Percy was astounded. Vesty was sprawled on the floor, Talula had returned to her human form and aside from looking exhausted seemed okay.

"We won then?" said Percy, rubbing his injured shoulder.

Smiling, Percy, Jimmy and Harry clutched each other in an awkward hug before hobbling over to Talula.

CHAPTER 31

With the blistering sun burning his neck, Will Potts looked up at the glorious, cloudless sky. He could feel the strap of his school bag digging into his shoulder. Will tried to shift the weight of the bag, but it slipped from his grasp and dropped to the floor jolting his body.

He sighed and for some reason, Jimmy Threepwood flickered across his mind.

Whatever happened to him I wonder? I've not seen him since that weird day in school and his father... I've knocked at his house a few times, but his mother says he not in and he's moved to a different school. I can't believe he's not phoned me. It's all very weird. I wonder if all this would have happened if I hadn't tackled Spike that day. I still don't know why I did it.

Will looked through the window of the house on the opposite side of the road and saw an elderly lady watching TV and stroking her cat. Just then Frankie Turnbull from school walked past.

"Alright, Potts?"

Will tilted his head back trying to look cool.

"Right, Frankie," said Will, and bent down to pick up his bag. He slung it over his shoulder. A double decker bus bobbed down the narrow road followed closely by two cars, which sent a wave of hot, dirty air over his face.

Adjusting the bag for comfort, Will took a step and realised that Frankie was gone. *That's weird,* he thought, and checked over his shoulder. *Where's he gone? What on earth? The cars have stopped as well?* Will felt anxiety growing in his stomach and walked on cautiously stopping to peek in gardens and houses but there was no one. The silence was starting to unnerve him. Glancing around, he realised that even the sky was empty, and the beautiful day had turned gloomy and dark. Will's breathing increased. *What do I do? What do I do? Drop the bag and run? No, that's silly. Alright calm down Will, it's nothing.*

His pace became brisk and he was alert as he walked past an empty street. His eyes were drawn to the path on the other side of the road. Resting on the concrete slabs was a long black sports bag, zipped closed, something was trapped inside and was kicking and moving about.

Will put his head down and walked on, until an invisible rope of conscience pulled him back. *What if it's a kid trapped in there? It's about that size—or a cat.*

"Errr," he shouted, crossed the road and tentatively approached the bag.

"Hello?" he shouted, poking the bag with his finger.

"Help!" A weak voice called back, and Will instinctively pulled away.

"Are you okay?" he asked.

"Help me, I'm stuck," the voice said again.

"Okay, Okay." *I'm gonna regret this,* he thought.

He pulled the little golden zip and opened the bag. A foul green goblin with long streaks of black hair burst out with its sharp teeth fully exposed. Before Will could move, the goblin hooked a golden necklace around his neck. Will felt its icy touch and his vision went black.

Standing tall, Xanadu circled her prize. Will's eyes glazed over, and Xanadu watched the magnificent blood red stone around his neck. It clouded and bubbled. The head of a sea green spirit floated out from the stone and hovered, its hair flowing in the summer breeze and its tongue licking its grubby moustache. Turning his eyes to the stagnant empty vessel before him the head surged into Will's gaping mouth. Will gasped, and his eyes shot open.

His eyes slowly rotated in all directions and a voice spoke.

A voice clearly not Will's.

"Xanadu. You have done well again. This boy, this Will Potts is the friend of Jimmy Threepwood. It will come as a great surprise to find his friend as the replacement for Lyreco, but I am sure it will keep him in line with our plans."

Will's body scrunched its fingers into a ball, then released them, a sliver of energy appeared, and he blew it into the air.

"My power is already coursing through his veins," said Lord Trident. "Soon I will have total control and he will be the perfect mentor for my Children of Tyranacus."

Xanadu brushed aside her tattered dirty brown cloak and knelt before Will Potts. "Yes, my master," she grovelled.

CHAPTER 32

The icy howling winds soared through Higuain's cowl, nearly tearing it from her head. She grabbed the end with the tips of her fingers and held it firmly in place. Taking her next step, her foot sank into the snow. She steadied herself and stepped forward again and a chill raced up her spine. She held her cloak tightly around her but could no longer feel the tip of her nose and her face felt raw.

Higuain narrowed her eyes, trying to find her way through the blizzard. She could barely see Stratos, Dravid or Shimmer, but she knew they were there. They had been walking for days along the snow-covered plains known as the Mountains of Wrath. They had rested for only a few hours each night, but the coldness had kept Higuain awake.

She felt her eyelids dropping with exhaustion. Giving in to the overwhelming feeling of tiredness, she closed her eyes for a moment, her head dropped forward, and jerked back awake. She opened her eyes, falling snow pelted her face and she felt the moistness on her cheeks, which were starting to freeze. She wiped her face with her hands and a spectral figure ghosted towards her at a great pace.

"Argonrrr," she sighed, stretching out her arms and releasing the cowl, which blew onto her back and flapped wildly in the wind. The vision had warmed her heart, which quickened and began to pump blood around her body.

As the apparition faded she stepped forward, her foot crashed into the ground and she lost her balance and toppled to the floor.

Dravid dropped to his knees and put his arms around her.

"You two, come over here!" he shouted to Shimmer and Stratos, and pulled them into a tight huddle, his arms around them as if they were in a rugby scrum. His arms liquefied and bubbled, and he fed heat into their weary bodies. After only a few minutes their bodies rejuvenated, and the warmth channelled through them.

"I know this is hard, but we must keep going. We must stay sharp. This place is home to Azzbecks and they can slash you in half with one swipe of their claws. You've all heard the stories." Dravid helped Higuain to her feet. "Come on, we must keep moving."

The snowfall eased and Dravid strained his eyes, trying to see through the white sheet ahead of them. In the distance he saw a smouldering igloo releasing a plume of black smoke high into the air. The thick rectangular ice blocks were charred, slowly losing their composition and he saw gaping holes in the ice, like the aftermath of an artillery strike.

In that instant he felt it … a presence lurking deep below them. His stomach went numb.

"Get down!" he screamed, and dived through the air tackling his three companions to the icy surface.

Two goliath claws erupted from deep below the snow slashing where their bodies had been only an instant earlier. An enormous white, fur-covered behemoth sprang up like a whale bursting through the ocean waves, landed on its two thick legs and thrashed ferocious claws wildly. It had two heads. Stratos stared up at the beast in horror. It roared, opening the mouths of its two huge heads and exposing enormous ivory fangs.

Stratos heaved himself up and pulled his axe from behind his back, "An Azzbeck!" he shouted as the snow and wind hurtled around him.

He raised his axe, gritted his teeth and swung with all his strength. Out of nowhere, Dravid struck his shoulder, causing the axe to miss the monster and the axe lodged deep in the snow.

"Wait! Just wait, let me see," said Dravid.

Without fear he stepped into the shadow of the beast. It towered above him so Dravid held his arms out making himself as big as possible. Suddenly the creature flinched and cowered, and in its haste to retreat it staggered and collapsed, crashing into the snow.

"Look!" shouted Dravid, pointing at the creature's side. "He's injured. I don't think he wanted to attack us. He was trying to defend himself."

Dravid knelt by the creature's side touching its soft fur. The monster stirred, opening its black pupils and groaned, muttering unintelligible animal sounds. Dravid placed the flat palm of his hand on its forehead and his eyes narrowed, the edges of his mouth curled over with concentration. Dravid's body liquefied, before slowly changing colour, thick white animal fur burst from every pore in his skin like a hedgehog before gradually returning to normal.

"Yen YAAAA!" he whispered, patting the creature's head. "Yen YAAAA!"

The creature responded in surprise and relaxed, closed its eyes and drifted off to a sleep.

"How do you know their language?" asked Shimmer.

"I didn't, but that is one of my gifts. With but a touch I can take a person or a creature's thoughts, their history, their language. It channels through my mind and the words make sense to me and my body adapts allowing me to say the complicated words that for example, a human couldn't. I remember when I met the Ineebry. Fascinating race, but to learn their language my jaw broke, realigned, then instantly healed." He adjusted his jaw bone to the right and poking his tongue out at a 90-degree angle and mumbled, "Gannnna zceee Goa."

Shimmer stared at him in dismay. The pronunciation sounded like he was choking on a boiled sweet. "That was their greeting ritual," Dravid continued. "Anyway, while I try to heal the injury, go to the damaged igloo and see what you can find. We will need a sled or some long planks, anything. I can heal him here, but the storm is starting to worsen again, and we'll need to find a shelter … and soon."

The blizzard intensified. Shimmer and Stratos returned dragging a sled across the snow.

"That's perfect." Dravid had to shout to be heard over the squealing winds. He had torn a large section from Higuain's cloak and used it to cover the creature's wound. Dravid gently rolled the creature towards him ready to slide the sledge underneath.

"The sledge was just outside the igloo. It was covered in crystallised berries and fruit. Whatever this is, it was out foraging for food," said Shimmer, pulling the beast's upper body onto the thin piece of wood with two skis attached to the bottom.

"And where are we going to take him? There's nowhere to go. It's just a mass of snow for miles," Stratos asked Dravid.

"There!" Dravid shouted pointing into the distance, "Smoke."

Pulling his hood half over his face he peered through the snow, the wind stinging his eyes. Dravid was right. In the distance just over a hill, smoke billowed from another igloo.

"I saw it while you were searching for a sledge. If we can get him there he can rest, and I think he will be fine."

Stratos nodded, he and Shimmer grabbed the reins and they pulled the beast through the snow and over the hill.

Stratos's biceps and shoulders were on fire. He turned to Shimmer. He watched the leather straps slip through Shimmer's fingers and he dropped the sled collapsing to his knees in the snow. Dravid stopped pushing from behind and quickly took his companion's arms.

"Are you okay? We're nearly there."

"It's my arms. They're burning, I'm in agony."

"Okay," Dravid said grabbing Shimmer's hands. His fingers liquefied, and a blue fluid drained into Shimmer's glowing skin then faded away.

Breathing out a cloud of air, he stood up flexing his arms and looked at Dravid like a miracle worker. "The pain's gone! My arms feel like new, how did you …"

Dravid cut him off, "Come on, we need to get him into the warm."

Stratos could see smoke rising from the roof, it was covered in black singe marks and thousands of tiny holes in the ice dripping onto the snow below.

He flagged the others, indicating that they should stay where they were, grabbed his axe and approached the igloo. He poked his head through the hole where the door should have been, and saw that the room was huge with blue lights dotted all around and long wooden benches positioned against the wall. With trepidation he walked in and jabbed a knee-high wooden cupboard with the end of his axe so that it rocked back and forth. The room was deathly still. Droplets of melted ice dripped onto his head from the multitude of tiny holes above. Despite the fact it was made entirely of sculpted ice, the room was surprisingly warm.

He moved back out into the cold and surveyed the area, then took hold of the leather reins of the sled. "There's no one here!" he shouted. "Let's get the creature inside and then we can get out of here!"

The air smelt of wet dog and it took nearly twenty minutes to drag the injured Azzbeck into the igloo and onto a wooden seat. Dravid checked the creature's wound again and picked up a woollen quilt from the floor in the corner of the room, which he used to cover his patient. The four companions then walked back out into the extreme, mountain weather.

CHAPTER 33

Dravid glanced back through the entrance of the igloo. A hint of regret played a merry tune in the back of his mind. It was against his code, his training, to leave anyone injured and uncared for, but he had to press on for Argon and the good of the world.

He turned his back on the igloo and strode forward but the ground below him suddenly started to shake. Six fierce Azzbecks ruptured the snow and burst upwards, landing one by one in a circle around the group. Screaming ferociously from their two fanged heads, thick snow tumbled from their fur, their hypnotising black eyes watched for the slightest movement.

Hissing and spitting, the creatures roared, swiping their claws at the group of travellers, who formed a combat pose with their backs to each other. Stratos gripped the handle of his axe tightly and for the first time could feel the fear rising deep within him.

The taller of the Azzbecks, one with greyer, fluffier fur and a brown streak running down his chest, screamed. The group stared as the two heads roared in unison. Standing tall, the Azzbeck violently beat its giant fists on its chest. It howled and slashed its claw knocking the axe clean from Stratos's hand.

Higuain's hands burst into fire and she thrust the flame towards the Azzbeck directly in front of her. To her amazement it whimpered and stepped back, putting its paws in front of its face and hissed like a frightened cat. Seizing her chance, Higuain quickly focused her mind and two rings of spinning fire ignited on the ground. One created a barrier between them and the Azzbecks and the other behind the Azzbecks prevented them from escaping.

The Azzbecks cried, stepping back from the fire, then jumped forward as their fur was singed by the blaze behind them. The creature with the brown stripe pushed his claws into the flickering light then yelped, yanking it away sharply. The creatures pulled their bodies in tightly, trembled as their fur stood up on end.

"They're afraid of us," Higuain said, releasing the outer ring of fire. The five Azzbecks scrambled past each other and scurried into the igloo, yapping as they ran. Brown Streak stood his ground still snarling and staring at the group through large black eyes.

"I think their bark is worse than their bite," Higuain said.

"Yeeee, Yo Laa," Dravid's voice shouted, pulling away from the circle and approaching the flame. The ground below his feet, near to the fire had turned to slush which splattered up his legs.

Brown Streak's focus shifted from Higuain to Dravid and it opened both of its mouths panting like a dog. Staring directly into its eyes, Dravid adjusted his jaw so he could pronounce the words correctly and said,

"ZZuuulooo Meee Arrr, Zemm Uoo Laa!" He thrust his arms out, in an introductory manner. "Uba MAnnnn, Killento. Milopento mmaaa. Ushbac leer," He tapped the side of his waist then pointed toward the still smouldering igloo.

"What are you saying?" asked Higuain.

Dravid didn't break his eye contact with Brown Streak and said. "It's okay Higuain, lower the flame. I've explained what we are doing here and how we have helped one of their injured compatriots."

Higuain waved her arms, the flames sank into the snow and the Azzbeck let out a groan and raised its paws high into the air.

"It's okay," Dravid shouted to his companions, "it's okay. He wants us to show him how we treated his son."

The creature marched on ahead through the snow. Dravid rummaged in his pocket and pulled out three shiny marbles, which rotated in his right hand. Moving them faster and faster he leant forward and breathed. A sparkling dust intertwined with his cold breath, and the particles clung to the meal spheres. The dust seeped into the balls and the colours faded to a dull grey.

Reaching out his hand and signalling his companions to take a marble, he spoke again. "I can instantly learn the language of any creature. Their past and the years they spent learning the words channel into my mind in seconds. These silver balls are known as Microtransters and allow me to feed my understanding of the language into them. When a creature speaks, the words spin around the inside of the sphere and amplify the language, which you understand. Carry them with you; you will need them to understand these primitive creatures."

Catching up to the Azzbeck leader they went into the warm igloo and were amazed to find the other five monstrous Azzbecks cowering in the corners.

"Arggh!" Brown Streak roared, "Stop whimpering! The intruders tell me they will not harm us. They have found and helped Fendor. Where is he?" His eyes opened wide when he saw the white furry creature lying still on the chair. Brown Streak moved to the injured creature and as he did the nails of his toes dug little divots out of the icy floor. Brown Streak knelt next to him and pulled up the quilt, gently touching the weeping bandage.

"My son," Brown Streak whispered, "I thought you were lost!" He pressed his small brown nose to the closer of his son's two heads and licked his fur. "When I heard your home had been attacked I sent out a pack of warriors to find you, but you were gone."

Stroking his son's head, Brown Streak stood up and turned to the group, a gentle purr in his voice. "Thank you, strangers, for finding and helping my son. Without you he would have certainly perished.

"My name is Lindor, and I am the leader of this Azzbeck pack. We are a peaceful race living in an area where there are very few visitors and even fewer guests. The Azzbeck you helped is my son, Fendor. We sent him out to look for food, but he never returned. His injury looks like some form of explosive spear," His facial expression hardened, and the purr was replaced by a growl.

"Is there any way the Azzbecks can repay this life debt to you? We will do anything we can."

"You son will be fine," said Dravid. "He will need rest, but he'll be fine. We have come to the Mountains of Wrath in search of the Granite Fairies. Do you know them? Have you heard of them?"

Lindor's face softened, he lowered his eyes, and turned to his pack one by one. They all nodded. "The Granite ...."

Shimmer flinched as a thunderous roar sounded overhead. The whole igloo shook with the sound of explosions high above them. Steam leaked from the ceiling and shards of ice and droplets of water fell to the floor. More noises rumbled overhead, and the tranquil white ceiling of the igloo turned into a blaze of fire.

Shimmer and Stratos ran out into the open air. A metal spear cut through the air and landed at their feet, burying in the snow. Higuain jumped towards them from the doorway and dragged the two men to the floor as the spear exploded, covering their bodies in ice and melted snow.

A blue bird with fierce eyes and exposed talons soared overhead dragging a small roman chariot sled through the air. A knee-high green goblin was holding the reins, its hands shaking from the intense vibration of the explosion. It wiped the shoulder length green Father Christmas style hat from its face and gave a vicious smile before pulling another spear from the bag behind him. The goblin yanked back the reins; the bird squawked and turned for another pass. The spear flew into the air towards the three warriors.

They scrambled to their feet and ran to the igloo as the weapon exploded behind them.

The goblin was joined by more of his army, who sent three more of the vicious javelin-weapons towards the ground. The spears detonated in the doorway. The impact cracked straight through the ice wall. Fragments of the structure fell to the floor and the igloo slumped sideways.

Shimmer ran outside and jumped through the plume of black smoke. One of the birds flew past catching Shimmer's shoulder with its claws. The chariot the bird was pulling crashed into Shimmer's back sending him flying through the air to land face first in the snow. Pulling himself to his feet Shimmer realised he was surrounded by at least seven of the goblin army circling high above him, all clasping spears in their hands. He could see the tips of the arrow heads shining, and he was trapped.

"You humans have chosen to help the Azzbecks! You will die as well as the Azzbecks." The goblin flicked the bobble on the end of his hat out of his eyes. "You are no match for the Granite Fairies and you will die first followed by those ... monsters." Shimmer was trapped. Whichever way he turned the goblins or self-named fairies were around him. He had nowhere to go, no means of escaping.

CHAPTER 34

"Why are they attacking you … us? What happened?" asked Higuain of Lindor.

Once again Lindor consulted his pack members. His eyes widened, and he started to purr. Higuain had the impression that Lindor was asking for forgiveness.

"The fairies think we have taken their ruler and master as a prisoner. They think we have broken the treaty set centuries ago."

"Well!" shouted Higuain. The monster took a step back in alarm.

"Urm, I think you should follow me," said Lindor, walking away.

Seven piercing, explosive spears sliced through the falling snow aimed at Shimmer. His heart rate and breathing intensified. Closing his eyes, he thought of home and in particular his father. Suddenly he felt his body tingle and the chilly air rushing past his face. He opened his eyes and his body was alight with silver glistening flames and he was flying high in the air. Below him an orchestra of explosions ruptured the ground. Seven of the angry fairies yanked on the reins of their chariots, skilfully controlling the mighty blue birds, and gave chase after Shimmer.

*   *   *

Lindor, followed by Higuain and Dravid, descended a dozen ice steps that were hidden behind a door in the igloo. The temperature around them had dropped dramatically. Lindor thrust his claws through the mist at a wall of solid blue ice—a barrel lock clicked, and a motor started turning and clanking. A thick slab of ice lifted, releasing a blast of compressed air into the small, cubed room.

There, frozen in the middle of a glowing crystal of pure blue ice, was a knee-high fairy. The fairy looked identical to the fairies that were even now raining fire and explosions on the igloo above them. The fairy was dressed in a bright floppy hat, a green suit and brown, knee-high boots.

"You did capture him," gasped Higuain.

"No, no, it's not what you think. He must have been flying on patrol when his Vortax bird crashed into a tree near here. One of foragers found him and he was gravely injured. We didn't know what to do with him and we have no medicine. The only thing we could do was freeze him in ice to preserve his body until the Granite Fairies could treat him. Before we had a chance to speak with them the hourly bombings started and ever since we have been too scared to leave the area.

"After a few weeks we ran out of food and my son, my brave, brave son, Fendor went out for food and never returned … until you arrived."

Dravid ran his hands over the ice. "They are right. He has an injury to his head and internal wounds. He'll need treatment and soon. I can feel his life force drifting away. Do the Granite Fairies have medicine? The means to help him?"

Lindor nodded. "Yes, I believe so, they are very advanced."

Dravid regarded Higuain with concern on his face. "We need to communicate with the fairies or he may not survive."

Higuain sighed, *we need these fairies* she thought. *They are the only ones who know where the Palletine flower is. I don't know how long Argon has left but we must resolve this and quickly before anything else happens.*

*   *   *

High above the igloo, Shimmer flinched, spears detonated all around him as he soared through the cold, misty air leaving a trail of silvery flames and angry Granite Fairies launching their onslaught.

In the distance the air began to change. It reminded Shimmer of gas waiting to be ignited. He put his head down and pushed forward through the quivering air and the instant he passed through, it ignited behind him in flames.

The fairies that had been pursuing him stopped mid-flight behind him, trapped by the flames. The flames had become a giant tube; the fairies were stuck in the middle of the spinning vortex of fire, with no exit. They screamed and threw spears at the tube, but they were simply sucked into the revolving field.

Far below him, Shimmer could see Higuain standing next to Lindor and Dravid. Higuain was concentrating with her eyes clenched and arms held aloft. He could see the strain in her face as her muscles twitched.

Landing on the on the snow and morphing back to human form, Shimmer saw Higuain using her hands to manipulate the tube and bring the flaming tube down to the ground. Higuain also reduced the size of the tube forcing the fairies that were trapped to remain completely still.

Inside the inferno prison the first fairy jabbed at the flame with his spear and snarled, "Humans! Why are you helping them? They have broken the treaty; they have stolen our Worshipful Master Nilingo. All we want is his safe return." He thrust the spear forward again. "The next squadron is due to strike soon and they will succeed where we have failed!"

Lindor took a step back.

With the strain evident on her face Higuain spoke, "Which of you is the leader of this squadron?"

The fairy poked at the flame again and hissed, "Me! I am the leader should Nilingo fall. I am the leader!"

"Then whom do I address?" she said.

"My name is Chaz. Why do you talk to us? Why have you not taken us captive?"

"Chaz, you seem to have your facts wrong. You are correct that the Azzbecks have Nilingo, but he is no prisoner. He crash-landed and was mortally injured. The Azzbecks are primitive and do not have the technology to heal him. He is safe and frozen within the shelter, but his time is running out."

"Lies!" Chaz said, agitated and suspicious. "Then why did they not tell us of these … facts."

"Because you didn't give them the chance! You have been doing nightly bombings for weeks. The Azzbecks have no food and this petty war will gain you nothing," Higuain spoke passionately.

Chaz rubbed the stubble on his chin. "Prove it. Take Dr Roman and me to see him, prove you're not lying and I shall call off the attack," he grabbed the closest goblin to him. "He is the Granite doctor. He will quickly tell me if you are telling the truth."

Higuain opened a small door in the flame tunnel and the two knee-high fairies stepped out suspiciously and walked across the snow following the others down into the room below the igloo.

On seeing the fairy in suspended hibernation, Dr Roman pulled a syringe out from his belt and injected it into the ice. He retracted a candescent fluid before holding it up to the light. Dr Roman flicked it with his finger then dripped a tiny amount onto his tongue.

Sighing, the doctor spoke. "They tell the truth, Chaz. He has internal and head injuries consistent with a crash or fall. I do believe that by freezing Nilingo they may have actually saved his life."

Chaz faced Higuain. "Will you allow us to treat him? To take him back to our village?"

Lindor roared and beat his chest. "He says yes!" Higuain said and smiled.

They climbed out of the room with the crystallised fairy and went back outside to the flaming tunnel. Higuain released her hold on the flame which released the other fairies and allowed her body to relax. Chaz was uneasy, scanning the area, suspicious of a trap or trick. The fairies gently dragged the frozen Nilingo onto one of their chariots.

CHAPTER 35

Jimmy ran to Talula, he could see that her robe was shredded, and she had cuts and bruises all over her face. Talula opened her eyes when she saw Jimmy and flung her arms around his neck. "I knew you would come for me. I knew you wouldn't leave me here."

Releasing him she slumped back weakly onto the steps.

"We need to get moving," said Percy, leaning against the wall.

"Not yet," said Jimmy, "we're exhausted and Talula can hardly stand."

"I know, but look!" said Percy.

Percy showed them the skin on his hands, which had turned a greyish sky blue. Percy pulled away his cloak to show them an injury on his left shoulder, and they saw that his skin was crumbling away and decaying. "It's on my leg as well. Once it had all calmed down my leg was throbbing. The potion that Shango Typariio gave us is wearing off. We need to find the Elixir and we need it fast."

Jimmy looked at his own hands and could see that they were also fading in colour. He pulled out the map that he had managed to keep hold of through his battle with Vesty. He ran his finger over where they were and where they needed to be.

"Here," he said, pointing to a spot on the map. "The Granite Fairies know the location of the Palletine flower and they live here in the Mountains of Wrath." The others wearily pulled themselves up and crowded around the map. "It's about a day's travel although maybe a little longer with Talula."

Harry sighed, rubbing his aching arm muscles and said, "Come on, we need to keep going, we will have to take turns helping Talula."

* * *

The morning sun rose quietly over the horizon on a beautiful calm morning. A deathly chill still floated in the air, but at least the snow had stopped. The four warriors had enjoyed the hospitality shown by the Azzbecks, staying the night in the igloo, but now they were refreshed, fed and watered and ready to recommence their journey.

In the distance a small figure approached casting a long shadow before him.

When he reached Lindor, Chaz removed his hat and bowed, keeping his eyes firmly focused on the snow-covered ground, "We, the Granite Fairies, have done you and your pack a grave wrong. We acted with anger and suspicion without allowing you time to explain the facts.

"I've come to ask you to consider renewing our treaty with the condition that in future we share greater communication and provide access for your species to our medical facilities. It would also give me great honour to invite the Azzbecks to a celebratory feast, since no one has been seriously injured during this foolish war."

A roar echoed from the igloo doorway. "Fendor! My son," Lindor shouted. "You have recovered." A smile spread across both Lindor's heads. The others could hear him purring, evidently pleased to see his son.

"Whilst we dine with you as our honoured guests I will provide an army of engineers to fix the homes that we destroyed, and in the future, we will become allies," said Chaz.

The knee-high green fairy only came to Lindor's shin, but he thrust his hand out to seal the deal. Lindor bellowed and grabbed the fairy in both of his giant clawed paws, pulled him high into the air and hugged him, covering him in snot and saliva.

When Lindor eventually dropped Chaz to the floor he wiped his face, gave a half smile, turned and walked towards Higuain.

Showing his teeth, Chaz said, "I'm afraid humans are still not welcome here. We have seen what you have done to this world and we wish to live in our sanctuary without your interference. However, I've heard you have travelled far to find us." They both started to walk toward the blazing morning sun. The others followed them slowly.

"I understand your reservations about my species and I will respect that," said Higuain. "We have sought you out and are in great haste to find the Palletine Flower. I've been told you are the guardians of the flower and the only people who know where it lies."

"You seek the Elixir of Light?" Chaz said, a smile on his face. "The legend passed down for centuries through cave paintings and works of art tell that one day a foursome will seek us out for that knowledge, but you are not what I was expecting. The images depict rage, hate, and destruction. Not the help you have provided.

"But alas," Chaz continued, "the time cannot be upon us yet, for we have no knowledge of the flower. It is clear from the paintings that someday soon we will have that knowledge but, as yet it has not presented itself."

Higuain could hear the fairy speaking but the words were a blur. They had travelled all this way and for nothing. Higuain pulled the map Jimmy had given her from her pocket and stared at it. She then turned it over, and stared again.

The disappointment was clear in her voice as she spoke. "But you are the guardians of the Palletine Flower? The flower that contains the blood of Velosaras?"

"I am sorry, Higuain," said Chaz. "That privilege and title will one day be ours, but not yet."

Higuain's heart sank. The world was spinning. She could feel her stomach churning and her breathing became shallow. *I can't save you, Argon, we are too early ... I'm so sorry.*

A hand grabbed her shoulder. A feeling of euphoria, warmth, and love flooded through her body. Higuain turned around to see Shimmer smiling back at her.

"Higuain, this can't be over. You received a message from Argon and Jimmy Threepwood also received it, why else would he risk giving you the map? The time must be soon."

"My friends," Chaz said, "why don't you come to my village? See the marvellous structures. It might provide inspiration for the next stage of your journey?"

The group had walked but a few miles when they felt the climate change. The air became warm and fresh and the ground was no longer snow-covered but hard and rocky. They walked on and found themselves in a village. They followed Chaz through the centre of the village, which was comprised of hundreds of tiny straw huts. Higuain was amazed that they were only a short distance away from the igloo, yet everything was completely different. There wasn't a sliver of snow in sight. The village was nestled in the shadow of a giant, jagged mountain rising high into the clouds.

Shimmer pointed beyond the mountains to where the sky was filled with a blanket of gorgeous, fluffy white clouds set against a backdrop of exquisite blue sky. Higuain longed to touch the beauty; the clouds looked thick enough to live on.

"Dazzling sight, isn't it?" Chaz said. "Why do you think we set our home here?"

Higuain regained focus. "May we see the art and cave paintings? Maybe we can help to find the flower?"

"Hmmm," Chaz groaned. "We are a race that allows time to catch up to us. But … I can see no harm."

They walked through the village and Higuain saw a crowd of fairies screaming and cheering. To their left sat twenty Vortax birds with their heads buried in a trough tied to a wooden frame.

"What are they doing?" Higuain asked Chaz, drawn to the large crowd.

"That? That is a criminal," Chaz said, his voice laced with fury.

Higuain approached the crowd; she towered over them and could see steps leading to a tall wooden platform with two vertical beams. In the centre was a large wooden wheel spinning around. Then she saw a man with a long dishevelled grey beard looking as tattered and worn as the clothes he wore. The man was tied to the spinning wheel and fairies were taking turns to throw spears at him. All the spears were intentionally missing him and imbedding in the wood surrounding his head.

"Have no fear. They will not hurt him. This is merely target practice," Chaz said.

"What did he do?" asked Shimmer, concerned.

"He is a thief. He is a lightning catcher who flies around stealing lightning from the air and selling it to bandits as weapons. But this is a peaceful area and he kept coming back and it was severely affecting our climate. It took us years to capture him, then a week ago imagine our surprise when he virtually fell into our laps."

Shimmer flinched as a spear buried into the wooden plate just next to the thief's shoulder.

"Come on, the caves are this way."

Higuain and Shimmer followed but Higuain had a nagging urge to turn around. Higuain stopped just as the wheel spun. With the spinning of the wheel the man became a blur, and while he was spinning Higuain thought she saw him change into Argon. The wheel slowed down, and she shook her head as the scruffy old man was still tied in place, but Argon was nowhere to be seen. Taking it as a sign, Higuain paid more attention to the contraption the prisoner was tied to and saw an engraved owl on the wooden plate above his head.

"Chaz!" Higuain shouted. "That contraption you are using there. Who made it?"

Chaz scratched his scaled nose, trying to think. "I don't remember. It's always been here. Come to think of it, it's in some of the cave drawings, so quite a while."

Higuain could feel her excitement growing. "How many times have you used it?"

Pulling a puzzled face, Chaz said, "Urm, never, come to think of it."

"It's him! The captive! He knows where the Palletine Flower is."

Higuain ran to the prisoner just as a fairy picked up his spear. Distracted, the fairy slipped, and the spear flew from his hand heading straight at the prisoner's head. At the very last second a gust of wind came out of nowhere and moved the wheel. The wheel adjusted the prisoner's position and the spear drilled into where his head should have been.

"No more spears! No more spears!" shouted Chaz.

Higuain continued to push through the crowd and jumped on the platform. Higuain cut the prisoner free and he dropped to his knees. The man was exhausted and barely conscious, but the sweet aroma of his rescuer revived him.

In a weak, croaky voice the prisoner spoke and gazed into her eyes. "We have met before." He reached out his hand to stroke Higuain's long brown hair.

"What is your name?" Higuain said, softly supporting his head.

"My name is Cryo Platt."

"Do you know where the Palletine Flower can be found?" Higuain asked.

The man smiled and said, "The Elixir of Light. Yes … I found it many years ago. Legend says it will only blossom once every two millennia. In the decade of Tyranacus. Once it is gone, it is gone … And it is ready."

"Will you take us to it?" Higuain asked, on the verge of exploding through excitement.

"That Higuain, is what happened in my dream," he said, and he closed his eyes to rest.

How does he know my name? she thought.

"Chaz, is there somewhere we can take him and treat him?"

"But he is a criminal!" Chaz replied. "If we help him he could destroy this area."

"Chaz!" Higuain said firmly. "This is it. Your destiny. You are the guardians of the Palletine flower. You need him to help you find the exact location then you can pass this knowledge down for centuries."

Chaz thought for a moment then beckoned to a nearby fairy. "Take him to the medical hut. We will treat him and help find the flower."

CHAPTER 36

On the outskirts of the village, Cryo pointed to a large grey rock camouflaged with tree branches and giant green leaves.

Behind the rock was hidden a wicker basket tightly woven together with four thin vertical metal poles in each corner. The basket was large enough to hold at least eight people and still have space. The group pulled away the leaves and branches to reveal a blue, rubbery deflated balloon. Kneeling next to it and rubbing his hands over it to flatten it out, Cryo shouted to Stratos, "Look in the basket. Can you see a cylinder? Rest it on the floor and pick the gloves and goggles up as well."

Stratos leant over the basket and fumbled around catching his arm on the big circular wooden steering wheel positioned directly in the middle of the basket. It was attached to the floor with wooden legs. Stratos studied the wheel and thought, *How is that wheel gonna work on this? It looks more like the steering wheel on a boat.*

Once Cryo had finished his preparations he checked the four poles on each corner of the basket, giving each one a good tug before saying, "You'd better stand back."

He pulled the thick black goggles down over his eyes and put the black rubber gloves on, pulling them up to his elbows. He grinned and dragged four copper wires from the cylinder and attached them to the four poles using metal alligator clamps.

When he turned the cylinder lid it hissed and sparked into life. Electricity crackled against the cylinder walls. As he rotated the handle again, the coils became rigid and a jolt of electricity travelled up the four posts and released its electrostatic discharge into the air. Cryo turned the lid to off, and the vibrating capsule he was holding became still. The four charged poles were swaying as the rubber balloon snaked over the floor and filled with air.

The balloon was ready to fly. The basket started to lift away from the ground. Grabbing the ropes, Cryo handed the capsule to Higuain.

"Get in!" he shouted to Dravid, Stratos and Shimmer. When the four of them were aboard Cryo released the rope and as it started to lift off he ran alongside and jumped in, spinning the wheel towards the mountain next to the village. Cryo pulled a white captain's hat from the floor of the basket, put it on his head and straightened the peak.

The balloon soared high into the air and the wind swept past their faces. Higuain asked Cryo, "Where are we going? Where's the flower?"

Cryo shouted to be heard above the howling wind, "There!" he pointed to the cloud circling the tip of mountain. "That's the entrance."

The fragile vessel creaked and jolted as it climbed up the mountain face. Reaching the summit, it ascended through a thick layer of unusual dense cloud, which felt like candyfloss covering their faces in a sweet sticky sugary substance.

The vessel stalled as it struggled to pull free from the glue-like texture but as it did they saw they were above a highway made entirely of soft, bouncy cloud shooting off as far as the eye could see.

"That's it! You need to follow the cloud path all the way to the end and that's where the Palletine flower grows."

"Can't you take us?" asked Higuain.

"I can't, I don't have enough juice left!" The group suddenly noticed that the balloon was starting to lose its shape. "I've just enough to get back down to the ground. I need to work out where the next lightning storm will start and travel to it. If I run out, I'll be stranded.

"That stuff is sticky but it's as strong as any road on the ground. I'll set you down just there. When you get the flower to this point, you can walk back down the mountain."

The basket hovered just above the ground so as not to get it entangled in the sticky substance. The four travellers jumped down. "All the best with your journey, Higuain. Thank you for saving me and I wish you all the best with Argon."

Cryo's hot air balloon sank back through the clouds. Shimmer tried to move his feet. He lifted his boot from the floor and a sticky chewing gum substance came with it. They all crouched down and touched the floor with their hands, but the cloud itself felt soft with a thin layer of white mist covering it.

"One of us will need to stay here," said Dravid. "This is an ocean of white and I don't think we'll find this entrance again."

"I'll stay!" shouted Shimmer. "This is your quest, you three have done this from the start and you should finish it together. I'll wait near here. Plus, if you do get lost I can fly to find you."

Locking forearms with Shimmer, Dravid nodded. "We will try to be quick."

*   *   *

Cryo guided the vessel gently back to the ground and it skidded along the rocky, uneven surface. Jumping out of the basket he tugged the rope and tied it to a tree before pulling out a map and an unusual square box with a dial that spun on the top. *Come on, stop spinning, stop spinning. I need this storm to be close. I've only got a small amount of power left. I'll be left stranded near the Pealanise Mountains knowing my luck.*

Cryo concentrated on the device until it finally stopped spinning. He looked up and was startled to see four black-robed children with glowing red eyes.

"Where did you just take Higuain and her companions?" Jimmy Threepwood demanded.

"Urmm, urm," stammered Cryos, 'they wanted to see the mountain. I took them to the top of the mountain. That's all."

"Lies!" the second boy shouted, placing his hand on Cryo's device. The metal box sizzled, and the glass case shattered. The casing melted, sending a waft of burnt sulphur into the air. With his hand glowing fiery red he spoke again, this time with menace.

"I won't ask again! Where did you take them?"

Cryo stuttered, "To find the Palletine Flower."

"Good," said Percy again. "So, you know where it is. You will take us there."

"I … I … I can't!" Cryo quivered. "Muh … muh … my ship doesn't have enough electrical charge. That's why I came here and used the Lightning Sphere." Cryo discarded the melted device onto the floor.

Jimmy studied the balloon and the four protruding poles still sparking an electrical current. Concentrating, two lightning bolt daggers formed in his hands, which he threw into the air. The bolts hit the closest poles and they exploded in a blaze of energy. The crackling discharge illuminated the farthest poles and travelled back along the Alligator teeth, the coils and into the cylinder.

With intensity the contents of the cylinder shone bright yellow and the power caused the ship to pull away from the ground nearly tearing the tree that is was tethered to from the earth.

Jimmy's eyes burned an image into Cryo's mind. "I assume this will be payment enough."

The four children climbed into the basket and began their ascent up the mountain.

The flying basket burst through the clouds.

*   *   *

Shimmer, who was still waiting at the entrance looked up at the rapidly approaching vessel. "Jimmy!" he whispered in horror, and morphed into the silver phoenix that blended into the thin layer of mist.

The four young warriors jumped from the ship. Shimmer looked on as Jimmy and Talula studied their hands with worried expressions on their faces. Cryo flew back into the air and disappeared into the distance. The four children of darkness followed the same path, which only moments earlier Shimmer had seen his friends walk along.

CHAPTER 37

Higuain walked with great haste over the sticky, fluffy surface, a thousand emotions twirling around her mind. She stopped and felt her heart leap into her mouth. In the near distance, magnified in the most beautiful twinkling yellow light she had ever seen, sat the Palletine flower. Breathing a sigh of delight, she thought, *Argon we've done it. We've found the flower, soon you'll be young again and we can be together*.

Higuain, Dravid and Stratos began to run toward the flower. The air in front of them started to mist, and then hardened into a white fluffy wall, which quickly spread the full length of the highway, blocking their path. The layers of the white wall swayed as though being blown by a gentle breeze.

Several layers of the wall shifted and fused together into a giant face covering the centre of the wall.

It opened its large piercing green eyes and Higuain instantly recognised it. She'd seen the facial features before, it was the same as the Granite Fairies in the village below.

Breathing deeply and speaking in a serene manner, the clouded head spoke.

"I am Unlin and I am the leader of the Granite Fairies. I've been the guardian of this mystical flower for over two millennia. For this time, I nourished it and felt its power waiting for the time to come … the time of its emergence. For once the Palletine Flower buds, my time on this earth is over and another will grow in my place and have the distinction of caring for this majestic blossom."

Taking in a breath, the face continued.

"Now, who are you three? The time is upon us and the flower has grown but I sense goodness within you, not pain and destruction. Why do you seek the Elixir of Light?"

Higuain knelt and bowed her head; she could feel her knee sticking to the surface.

Bowing her head, she said, "Unlin, oh guardian of the flower, my name is Higuain and these are my faithful companions, Stratos and Dravid. We seek the power of the flower, just a mere drop to save our friend Argon. He survived …" A lump grew in her throat. She swallowed hard and coughed the next words. "He survived the destruction by Tyranacus. He survived to form an army to prevent it happening again, but he needs the Elixir. He needs the Elixir soon."

"I can feel he is more than a friend, Higuain, much, much more. I am the guardian of this flower, but my only role was to ensure its survival, a gardener you may say. I can feel my time is over. The people in search of the flower are here and my successor is ready."

The layers of cloud within Unlin's face started to separate, and before their eyes he withered and aged. Cracks of air started to form in the wall and bright light shone through.

"At last I am freeeee." Unlin sighed, the cloud wall diluted, and the face drifted gently into the air leaving the passage ahead clear.

Higuain took a step forward but the centre of the cloud highway also disappeared leaving a giant hole leading all the way down to the village below. With a blaze of light Higuain saw a creature or person being dragged up into the air from below and sucked through the cloud.

"Chaz?" Dravid asked, his mouth open.

Suspended in the air, the hole closed around Chaz's body, which remained still, in the shape of a star. His eyes glowed yellow and he spoke with a voice not his own.

"Higuain, you were correct. We were not ready to know the location of the Palletine Flower until the time was right and that time is here. Through these new eyes I can see the history of the flower, the history of the world. My form in this new world will grow here and once Unlin's flower is picked and dies I will start my assignment and care for the seed for another two millennia."

"But you aren't the leader of the Granite Fairies, are you? Nilingo is the leader."

Layers of cloud started swirling and forming around him. "Nilingo is injured and the time is now. For soon the flower will die and the fertilisation must begin."

With his last word he was covered in the fluffy, gooey substance. The wall expanded piece by piece and his body disappeared into the mist.

"Beee careful Light Dwellerrrrrrrs, for you are not allloooone."

Higuain watched Chaz vanish into the clouds and felt the strong grip of Stratos's hand on her shoulder.

"Come on, Higuain. Let's get that flower before the wall grows back."

Higuain climbed up the small bank of cloud and thrust her hand through the yellow light toward the flower. Tiny particles tickled her forearm and she felt the hairs on her neck tingle and stand on end.

She clipped the edge of a delicate leaf and a piece of the cloud highway to her left exploded in a plume of white smoke. Spinning around, a sizzling yellow lightning bolt fizzed past her face and dug into the ground electrifying the floor. The floor was alive, crackling and spluttering and turning a black angry colour. The air around them felt damp with the distinct smell of an approaching storm. The cloud highway shook beneath their feet and droplets of water poured out onto the unsuspecting villagers below.

* * *

When the first beads of water hit the floor below, the villagers raised their eyes to the grey sky. One piece of cloud in particular was vibrant with electrical charge. The rainfall intensified and a wailing wind swirled around their homes casting the area into darkness.

* * *

Stratos gripped the leather handle of his axe, the wind ruffled his red hair and he sneered at the four hooded demons approaching with their eyes burning fiery red. Higuain swept her cloak behind her back and stood alongside the wild man, ready for war.

"Why are you here?" demanded Talula. "That flower is meant for us!"

Harry charged at the trio standing their ground.

"Harry, wait!" screamed Talula. "Why do you always do that? Don't you ever learn?"

Harry discharged a blast of dark magic, sending a streak of light through the air. Stratos raised the flat side of his axe, which took the impact of the strike and caused him to stagger backwards. The energy channelled through his weapon and soaked into his arms.

Infuriated by the ease at which his attack was stopped, Harry let loose a second and third stream of light. Holding the axe in front of him Stratos held off the strikes. The intense power from Harry's attacks slowly drained from the axe into Stratos' arms. The power was seeping into his body and his boots sank into the sticky floor.

Stratos could feel the power circulating through his arms. He had never felt such evil. Gritting his teeth Harry approached Stratos at great speed. Stratos pulled the axe and power tightly into his chest; he could feel the power screaming to be released. As Harry stepped into range, Stratos pushed his axe and shot the power out with all his might, unleashing a tidal wave of built up energy, which engulfed Harry and sent him soaring through the air. Harry crashed further down the cloud onto his back.

Talula fashioned a sphere of green fire and launched it at Higuain. With a thrust of her hands the outline of a shield of fire formed, absorbing the blast. Gesturing with her hands, Higuain created a ring of fire around the children of Tyranacus.

Percy crouched to the floor, smirking. He leaped to his feet and released a gust of air to extinguish the flames. The force of the air ruffled through their robes and hair.

Talula and Jimmy charged forward but Percy yelped in pain as if a thousand pin point needles were stabbing his left leg. He dropped to the floor as fire ravaged his leg. The skin around his wound began peeling off his leg. Percy dragged himself along the floor, pulled himself to his feet and hobbled towards Jimmy.

Jimmy circled the mammoth man mountain and moved his fingers. A sword of lightning hissed into his hand. He slashed the sword and it collided with Stratos's axe and the impact reverberated through the air. The noise fell to the villagers below who dived into their houses for cover.

Jimmy and Stratos crashed their weapons together again locked in a battle of strength. Stratos pushed Jimmy away with ease but Percy appeared with hands doused in flames. Stratos ducked, kicking Percy hard on his exposed left leg. Percy screamed, dropping to his knees and Stratos raised his powerful axe and hit him full force with the flat side. Percy landed a great distance away unconscious, hidden by a layer of mist.

CHAPTER 38

Talula saw Dravid lurking near Jimmy so she created a toad warrior, which grew from the cloud and marched forward with its sword and shield swiping through the air in Dravid's direction.

Talula's hands were sparkling green and her shredded, robes flapped in the breeze. Higuain's long, mousy coloured hair flowed around her. She stared intently at the demon preventing her from saving Argon. Higuain moved her arm and Talula flinched, ready for action. Higuain could see the anger in Talula's eyes, the hatred, and the monster trapped within.

Thrusting forward Higuain released a ball of fire. Talula lifted her hand and upon impact the ball of fire disintegrated in a fizzle of air.

A sinister grin spread across Talula's face. "Argghhh!!" she screamed and generated a burst of power, unleashing it into Higuain's body. Higuain focused to enable a circular shield to ignite on her arm, but the impact blasted through the shield catching her square in the chest and she was thrown into the air.

Stratos hammered down with his axe just as Jimmy held up his lightning sword. The weapons sizzled. Stratos wrenched the entangled weapons apart, striking again and again and the force slammed Jimmy to the floor. Jimmy valiantly held his weapon in front of him, but he was now on his knees.

Talula slowly walked to her injured opponent and using an invisible levitation grip, swept Higuain from the floor and raised her high in the air. Higuain desperately kicked her legs and tried to pull herself free.

Talula turned her head back to see that Jimmy was on the floor holding his sword in the air while Stratos continuously pounded downward with all his might.

"Jimmy!" she screamed, and dropped Higuain who crashed to the floor. The air swirled around her like a twister and releasing her hands, the full force of Talula's powers discharged towards Stratos who was completely unaware of his new opponent.

Jimmy watched Talula drop Higuain and saw her now releasing a ball of energy on to Stratos. Stratos's body jerked and his eyes clouded over. The giant rocked on one leg, his axe fell to the floor and his body collapsed.

Jimmy pulled free his sword and stabbed it into the axe handle, pinning it to the floor. His hands sparkled into life and he thrust a thousand volts of electricity into Stratos's body. Then he pulled his hands away and collapsed.

Talula walked up the small mound of cloud to the flower. The closed bud reacted to the change in temperature and opened its head revealing a stem and four fist-sized red berries covered in black blotches. Talula tugged at the berry and it came loose. The texture felt hard, yet malleable, waxy. She put the head of the berry into her mouth and squeezed firmly. The juices exploded out and trickled down her throat.

Harry stumbled to his feet and put his arms around Percy. Hobbling to the flower they too snapped off the fruit and drank the nectar-like juice.

Jimmy was standing over Stratos breathing shallowly on the floor, his body was still smouldering.

"I didn't mean to do that," Jimmy murmured, staring at his hands as though they belonged to someone else. Higuain coughed then turned onto her side and crawled towards the flower.

"Jimmy, come on!" shouted Talula. "The flower is ready."

Jimmy could see an orange glow emanating from his friends' pores. The cuts and bruises on Talula's face and arms slowly closed then faded. Percy was standing up, putting his weight on his leg and his skin had refreshed to its normal colour and then there was Harry. A red vapour of electric light ran through his body sparking out of the ends of his fingertips. Harry gave the most maniacal smile, which sent a shiver down Jimmy's spine.

Higuain had dragged herself along the floor to lie at Jimmy's feet.

"Ppppleeasse, Jimmy," she said faintly, "plleeeassse, Argon only needs the tiniest drop."

Jimmy could feel butterflies doing backflips in his stomach. He stared at Stratos, then at Dravid being held at the tip of the toad warrior's sword. Thoughts drifted through his mind.

The old man waiting in Blackskull Mountain.

"Jimmy, we are the same ... because there is good pulsing through your blood" ... *his father made of glass telling him to meet Higuain ... Handing her the map in Black Friars Alley.* His mind was spinning when the words of Professor Tinker were thrown into the mix; *"A single drop of the blood will refresh your skin and return your youthful complexion, but to gain the ultimate surge of energy and set you on your way to unlimited power, you will need to drink the entire amount of*

the fluid for this will help your cells regenerate and allow you to sustain the greater creatures within the scrolls."

I need to take it all, he thought, running his fingers over his mouth.

Jimmy gazed deep into Higuain's eyes and could see she was being torn apart by this decision. Then it flooded into his mind ... the memory he could never forget, the memory of the lone female paramedic in his father's bedroom, shaking her head on that day. The day that changed his life forever. Anger boiled through his veins and along his muscles and his eyes changed into an even darker, bloodier colour red.

"I will become more powerful than anyone!" he screamed. "More powerful than anything; and I will destroy the Gatekeeper for what he did to me!"

Bounding forward he snapped off the berry and without a moment's hesitation burst it into his mouth; he felt the thick, gooey substance drain down his throat. *"Nooooo Jimmy, what have you done!"* his father's voice screamed into his mind. *"What have you doneeeeee?"*

Jimmy could feel his cells regenerating and his body became stronger, more powerful, surging with dark energy. He waited. and waited, but the anger and pain didn't disappear; it remained and suddenly increased tenfold, tormenting his mind.

Higuain watched in horror. The knee-high green plant withered, changing from a luscious, vibrant green to dirty brown, then black before it turned to ash and disappeared, floating into the air. Higuain's face showed her torment. Her body drooped, and Jimmy knew he'd crushed all her hope and that all was lost.

"This was Argon's only hope," Jimmy watched her world crashing. "What are we going to do? How can I save you now?" she whispered.

Talula, Percy and Harry laughed victoriously. Percy transformed into the blue and yellow dragon. Talula, Harry and Jimmy climbed on to the dragon, which took off from the cloud and flew towards the horizon. Jimmy sat at the rear of the dragon, his hands firmly holding Talula's waist.

He looked back over his shoulder to the remains of the flower and then at Higuain. His eyes faded back to their natural brown colour and a solitary tear trickled down his face.

*　　　*　　　*

Higuain forced herself to her feet, keeping pressure on her chest where the blast had hit her. She staggered along before crouching down next to Stratos. Tears streamed down Higuain's face and she stroked his singed unkempt wild hair and stroked his beard. Stratos wearily opened his eyes and Higuain whispered, "It's over. They've won."

She turned to Dravid who had also crawled over to Stratos. Dravid was already beginning to heal the wounds that the mighty warrior, Stratos, had received.

Higuain could feel tears welling up. With a long deep sigh, she stood up and felt a gentle breeze brushing her face.

The breeze grew more intense, the air thickened to form a cloud, then another, then another. The mound of clouds merged and a face she recognised slowly developed.

"Chaz!" said Higuain, happy to see a friendly face. "Is that you?"

"My dear Higuain," Chaz echoed, "this is all that is left of me. This tiny piece of my mind. But I can help yooooou!" The cloud sailed delicately through the air hovering high above the mound where the plant had been. "For I am the gardener of this sacred ground!"

Chaz's spiritual form dived into the mound. With a gentle rumble a tiny green bud sprang from the ground, and a yellow spotlight magnified the area. High in the distant plains Chaz could be heard groaning in pain, breathing heavily. Another flower had taken root and grown from the mound.

"Another Palletine Flower!" said Higuain, in amazement.

She ran to the flower, pushed her hand through the light and it instantly reacted, revealing a solitary dark red berry, a quarter the size of the others. Snapping the fruit off the flower she stepped backward. Chaz breathed out as if releasing a great strain and the flower bud vanished.

"Go. Go quickly!" Chaz shouted. "My form is gone, and I am losing control. Go before the process is finished and you are stuck here."

Higuain clutched the berry to her chest and smiled.

"Thank you, Chaz. I'll never forget this!" Higuain ran to help Dravid with Stratos. Dragging him to the wall, which was fully formed, they spied a small doorway being held open. The door was beginning to close, so they moved quicker and with a final dive shot through the gap. The cloud wall slammed shut behind them.

They tumbled through the door and landed in a heap on the floor. Higuain detangled herself from the other two. She held the red berry aloft and shouted, "We've got it! We've got it!" Then she allowed herself time to relax in the soft, sticky clouds. She could hear shouting behind her, so she placed the berry inside a glass jar that she carried attached to her belt, and looked into the air. An electric-charged balloon floated over her head and dropped an anchor into the cloud floor.

The balloon landed awkwardly on the cloud. Shimmer and Cryo Platt jumped out of the balloon and ran to Higuain, Dravid and Stratos. Shimmer's feet touched the ground and he was different. His body was rejuvenated and the three deep claw marks that had mysteriously appeared on the right side of his face three days earlier had healed …

Cryo spoke, "I'm sorry! I had no choice, they made me bring them here, but I went to get help and then I saw Shimmer. We went to the Azzbecks for help, but only one of them was brave enough to help."

A roar came from the balloon basket and a huge, two headed, white furry beast climbed out.

"Fendor!" Dravid said in greeting.

On seeing the group of warriors Fendor roared again. this time beating his chest. Cryo spoke. "Fendor wanted to thank you for saving him and would like to pledge his allegiance to your Army of Light Dwellers."

CHAPTER 39

The Gatekeeper scratched the bony remains of his gruesome fingers down the grand mirror and watched the events on the cloud unfold. The squealing noise sent a tremble through the wasted souls that surrounded his lair, and they grabbed their ears and screamed in distress.

"So, Jimmy Threepwood, you have found the Elixir of Light and once again you dare threaten me?!" The Gatekeeper's voice grew angrier and his straining nails pushed forcefully against the mirror. The mirror cracked under the pressure sending a scar diagonally across the reflective surface.

"Soon it will be time to put your skills to the test!" the Gatekeeper declared.

Sniffing the air, the Gatekeeper's anger dissipated and smiling he turned. On the release of his grip, the remaining glass in the mirror shattered into a hundred pieces on the floor.

The Gatekeeper strolled to the centre of the room, kicked a black shadowy hand out of the way. The hand had over-stretched onto the path as its owner begged for release.

The Gatekeeper chuckled, sensing a new arrival. "I've been waiting for thousands of years for you. I've a special place in my sanctuary for your torment."

The air in front of him distorted and a large purple door opened. Vesty was shoved through still bleeding from his chest. The instant his feet touched the scorching cavern floor, four flaming chains shot out from the wall and fastened tightly around his ankles and wrists. A black shadow screamed in pain and engulfed his giant bat-like wings and feet before slowly crawling up to his waist then covering his arms and neck.

The Gatekeeper approached Vesty, running his sharp fingernail down his face.

Vesty spluttered, his lungs crushed by the invisible force the Gatekeeper was using. Wearily he opened his eyes and spoke, "There is still another who can release Tyranacus. Another that can still destroy yooouu."

The Gatekeeper flung aside his cloak and glided away.

With a yank of the chains Vesty was dragged screeching through the room, knocking the other souls aside as the orange-red flames of his new cell billowed to the ceiling in glee at a new prisoner to torment.

The Gatekeeper stared at the black velvet backing of the shattered mirror, all that was left on the frame. Within the darkness of the cavern a pair of yellow eyes illuminated.

A dark, sinister voice, spoke. "Everything is going to plan, Gatekeeper. The council will suffer for what they have done to you and we will form the new world together as planned. Soon we will be ready for the next stage. A stage that will make Jimmy Threepwood and his companions wish they never left their ordinary, pathetic, lives!"

"Yes," snarled The Gatekeeper. "Everything is going as planned." The Gatekeeper glided away to find another soul to torment. As he left the hundreds of shards of shattered mirrored glass lifted into the air and reformed the mirror, remaking its liquified texture.

The mirror sprang to life showing the image of Higuain pouring the Elixir of Light into Argon's mouth. The mirror and room fell into darkness; all that could be heard were the howls of pain and suffering in the Gatekeeper's cavern.

The adventure continues in:

Jimmy Threepwood and the Echoes of the Past.

Thank you for choosing this book. If you enjoyed it, please consider telling your friends or leaving a review on Goodreads or the site where you bought it. Word of mouth is an author's best friend and much appreciated.

About the Author

Rich Pitman is originally from Newport, South Wales. He is the author of the children's fantasy series, Jimmy Threepwood, starting with The Veil of Darkness and followed by the second book, Jimmy Threepwood and The Elixir of Light.

Rich is a member of the Society of Children's Book Writers and Illustrators (SCBWI) and Literary Wales.

https://www.facebook.com/jimmy.threepwood
https://www.linkedin.com/in/rich-pitman-3427bb5b
https://www.goodreads.com/author/show/64399938.Rich_Pitman
Twitter-- @threepwoodbooks
https://pinterest.com/jimmythreepwood/
http://jimmythreepwoodblog.wordpress.com/
http://www.peoplesbookprize.com/section.php?id=7

Also by Rich Pitman

Jimmy Threepwood and the Veil of Darkness

Even heroes do bad things, but there's something really unfortunate about being selected to join the forces of evil and become one of the four horsemen of the apocalypse!

When Jimmy Threepwood is collected to face his dark destiny and destroy the world with his supernatural powers, he is faced with a choice ...

What lengths will he go to for the sake of revenge?

ROGERSTONE

8/10/20

X034142

CPSIA information can be obtained
at www.ICGtesting.com
Printed in the USA
LVHW051505010819
626171LV00011B/518/P